Escapade
Her Billionaire – London

LISA MARIE RICE

Escapade ©2018 by Lisa Marie Rice

Published by Lisa Marie Rice

Cover Design & Formatting
by Sweet 'N Spicy Designs

Acknowledgments

Many, many thanks to Judith Edge, who made this book so much better.

And a shout out to Richard and Esther Hooley, who provided information on Ferraris and the Thames. The cool stuff is theirs, the mistakes are mine.

One

She was a looker.

Really gorgeous in a punk schoolmarm-y kind of way. Not that any of the males in the room would notice. There was very little testosterone in this room of two hundred math geeks, most of them guys. More or less all the testosterone in the room was his, and it was sitting up and taking notice.

Not good.

Bennett Cameron wasn't used to having testosterone released during a job for anything but aggression. He was a close protection expert — a bodyguard, in civilian terms — and he was used to being alert to anything that could be a source of danger. When on the clock, his body was flooded with testosterone and cortisol, the arousal and stress hormones. Arousal as in all systems go, every sense up and run-

1

ning, including the sixth one.

Not arousal as in a hard-on.

He'd been a security consultant long enough to have a sixth and even seventh sense for danger. Nothing got by him.

Right now, nothing was pinging on his danger radar so all that testosterone went to one special part of his body, watching the lithe young beauty parade across the stage, mouthing mathematical formulae, following abstruse lines of thought, of which he understood one word in ten.

Still, he didn't have to understand her math. He just had to keep her safe.

But first he had to kidnap her.

That was a royal pain in the ass. And maybe not easy, either. Bennett watched her on the stage, pacing back and forth, elaborating some incredibly long and complicated thought that had the audience gasping, then tittering, then sighing. Whatever she was saying — and he had no hope of deciphering it — was a real hit with the geeks.

But where the geeks and nerds all looked lost, with their too big sweaters that looked like their moms had dressed them in expectation of that last spurt of growth, cumulatively smelling a bit rank, completely engrossed in what she was saying, the woman herself, Dr. Eleonore Castle, known by her peers as E. M. Castle for Eleonore Marion Castle, known by her friends as Elle, seemed very alert. Very aware of her surroundings. Those cobalt-blue eyes as she looked around the room seemed very very sharp.

She looked pretty unkidappable if he wanted to keep it calm and quiet.

He was at the back of the room, hiding behind a pillar. The stage lights were in her eyes. There was no chance that she could see him, but still he stuck to the shadows, biding his time. There was no way he could abduct her in front of two hundred geeks.

Well actually he *could* … given the fitness level of the audience. But they would all surely have cellphones and a robust virtual life more interesting than their real lives, so the scene of Dr. Eleonore Castle being abducted in the civilized confines of the Mathematical Institute of Oxford University would explode and go viral on all social media in about five seconds.

Bennett's company operated below the radar, which is why it was so successful. A media frenzy would be bad for this op in particular and terrible for his company in general. Not to mention it would paint a huge bullseye on the good doctor's very pretty back, when he'd signed a million-dollar contract to protect that back. And front, for that matter.

Her talk was a long one but fascinating, to judge by the rapt expressions of the audience. Bennett himself didn't have a clue.

"And then one could just camp out on the x axis forever, am I right?" she said, bafflingly, and even more bafflingly, the whole room erupted in chuckles.

Well, he wasn't going to kidnap her in the auditorium, and what she was saying was nonsense to him, so he had best use the time in research. He was as good at research as he was in Close Quarters Combat and Close Protection, which was why his company had taken off.

Okay. Nothing like St. Google to give you info and … oh wow. Pages and pages and *pages* of stuff on Dr. Castle. If you googled his name, Bennett Cameron, you'd get a few very spare returns and a tripwire in one of his back offices would send him a message that someone had pinged him. Bennett operated way under the radar.

But the people with the money to afford him knew about him and knew how to get in touch with him.

So, the very pretty doctor had academic credentials as long as his dick. A doctorate and two masters and a number of seminars that she both attended and taught. A list of publications that was impressive for someone so young, including two books. Wait — he didn't know how old she was. Her father hadn't told him. And she looked really young up there on the stage. And she had a doctorate and two masters and all those courses, so how the hell —

Oh. She went to Harvard when she was fourteen. Damn.

A lot of brain power in that pretty head.

Bennett looked at what she'd been doing the past six months. Most people were creatures of habit and if you wanted to know where they were and what they were doing, your best bet was to check where they'd been and what they'd done.

Conferences all over the place, with strange names. Behavioral Economics, Mechanism Design, Circuits and Systems. Conferences in Berkley, Singapore, St. Petersburg, Las Vegas, Guangzhu, Abu Dhabi, just in the last six months alone. The woman got around.

This was not a bad thing. He could pass for a math nerd for about ten seconds and say they'd met at a conference. She couldn't possibly remember everyone she met when she was on the road so much.

So that was the play.

Catch her after the symposium, tell her they'd met in wherever, whenever, get her in a quiet space, explain about her father, whisk her away.

Done deal.

So Bennett waited patiently for her to finish her incomprehensible talk and tried not to let his mind wander. Someone in close protection never let their mind wander, ever. Intense vigilance while on the job was a prerequisite. Lose focus for a second and you could lose a life.

But right now, there was nothing to do and there was no imminent danger so he could relax his vigilance, just a bit.

He had a perfect view of the main entrance to the auditorium. There was a small hidden door behind the podium, too. Nobody could come in without him seeing who it was. If anything happened in the auditorium itself, if anyone stood up to shoot her, Bennett would shoot him first. He and his company worked often for the UK government and he had been granted a license to carry in the UK. He was an excellent shot. A former sniper, in fact.

So Bennett kept an eye on the beauty up on stage with a part of his head thinking in non-tactical terms.

Slender, long-limbed, agile. She paced gracefully as she unwound a long, involved line of reasoning that took up three slides of dense math on the screen. Bennett lost track immediately.

Man, she was just amazing. Particularly considering that her father, Clifford Ricks, resembled a toad. Eleonore or Elle or Ellie was the man's only child, fruit of his first marriage. The old man had gone on to five more marriages, each divorce costing him more than ten million dollars. Luckily, he had money to spare.

She was wearing a jacket that could only be described as post-modern. Cut askew, it was both weird and attractive because it hugged her slender curvy figure and it was a deep brilliant cobalt blue that exactly matched her eyes. And she was wearing tight, stovepipe black pants that exactly matched the color of her hair.

Bennett didn't often get a chance to admire who he was protecting, not in this way. He'd protected beautiful women before, usually the wives of rich men, their minds as empty as their faces were beautiful. Though, to tell the truth, he didn't do much close protection himself these days. He had men for that. A hundred and fifty of them, to be exact, all of them hand-picked.

It was a young man's game and though Bennett wasn't old, he wasn't young any more either. Too old for this kind of work. His company was moving into more intel-dense work, finding missing people, tracking down money launderers, that kind of thing.

He'd only accepted this contract because Clifford Ricks had begged him. Saying he'd get on his knees if he still could. Ricks's hedge fund had thrown millions of dollars' worth of work to Bennett's company and, well, a young woman in danger. It wasn't in him to refuse.

And now that he'd had a glimpse of the daughter, he was more glad than ever that he'd accepted the job.

Clifford Ricks's enemy was Anton Lipov, who headed an offshoot of the Volcic mob, known for its extreme cruelty. They placed their enemies on a meat hook and watched them die, over the course of days.

That wasn't going to happen to Elle Castle.

Whoa. The talk was over. Elle took a little sardonic bow as the auditorium rose, clapping.

Fuck. They all looked eager to rush to the podium to grab a bite of the star. Bennett couldn't protect her in a crowd, not without showing his hand and it was too early for that. He moved forward, running through scenarios in his head, when she suddenly ... disappeared.

What the hell?

The hidden door behind the podium clicked shut. She'd escaped out the back of the stage. Well, Bennett couldn't fault her. The smell of unwashed clothes and a few whiffs of major halitosis were detectable even at the back of the auditorium. He could only imagine how repulsive the nerds would be up close and personal. But now he was going to have to be fast to catch up with her.

He knew how to move fast without appearing to rush. He had long legs and he lengthened his stride without moving his upper body much. In a few seconds he was out the door and into the big hallway. The original building was ancient. He had no idea how ancient but it boasted spires and and flagstoned floors and stained glass windows. The math annexe was modern, though, with acres of carpeted hallways.

Bennett quartered the area without swiveling his head, without making it obvious he was looking for someone. There were three directions she could have gone and he studied each one carefully.

There! Making her way down the hallway which was the fastest route out of the building. And man, she was making tracks.

Bennett lengthened his stride even more. "Elle! Ellie! *Elle Castle!*" he called out behind her, relieved when she slowed and turned around.

"Hey!" Bennett put on his genial good guy face. He'd trained to kill since he was eighteen and he'd killed twelve men in battle and three in close protection. When he wanted to, he could switch to his war face and it was frightening. But he could also smile and look as harmless as someone built like him could look. He pasted a delighted smile on his face. "Good to see you! That was a really interesting talk back there."

Bennett wasn't a ladies' man, but he also wasn't bad looking and he knew how to charm the ladies when he had to. But Elle wasn't having it and was definitely not charmed. She stared up at him and it was like being caught in the beam of twin cobalt spotlights.

"Do I know you?" she asked, voice cold.

He plastered a hand over his heart. "You wound me, you really do. We shared a glass of indifferent champagne at the reception in St Petersburg. The caviar was good, though."

Her eyes searched his face. "No," she said flatly, "we didn't. I've never seen you before in my life."

Oh man. God save him from smart women with steel trap memories. She also seemed pretty impervious to his charms. Bennett took her arm gently, hoping to walk her closer to the exit door while trying to convince her they'd met before. He remembered the name of one of the authors of a paper.

"Surely you haven't forgotten Leontov too? And his dandruff?" Since the guy was a mathematician, it was a pretty good guess that he had dandruff. Unless he was completely bald. It was a 50-50 shot.

Eleonore Castle dug in her heels. To move her

now he'd have to use at least a minimum amount of force. And she'd probably raise a fuss. They were surrounded by people. She looked pointedly at his hand on her elbow. "I'll thank you to stop manhandling me and to leave me alone, otherwise I'm calling security."

Well, she could hardly know that he'd easily deal with a Brit rent-a-cop. Or even several of them.

But they were wasting time on a very time-sensitive mission. Bennett stifled a sigh. He looked down into her beautiful angry mistrustful face and took an executive decision.

"Sorry, darling," he murmured. "I really don't want to do this, but I have to."

And he injected her with a fast-acting psychotropic drug that would make her amenable but not unconscious. She gave a small cry at the slight sting of the needle then, after a moment, her eyes unfocused.

Bennett waited a few seconds for the drug to take effect. He wasn't happy about it. He was a good guy and he was saving her life but man, he didn't like drugging a woman. But she was too smart for her own good, so what choice did he have?

"Come on, darling," he said and took her arm again.

She shambled forward obediently.

Two

Elle Castle came to slowly, like rising up from the bottom of the ocean. Rocking in the water, coming slowly up into the light. It made her seasick. She swallowed heavily, opened her eyes, then closed them again.

There was something … some*one*. Right in front of her. A man she'd never seen before or … maybe … maybe she had.

Nothing was certain except that she felt like she was in a boat, rocking on troubled waters and that her head hurt, with a sharp pain she'd never felt before. Like a nail spiked into her head.

"What's going on? Where am I?" she said. Only it didn't come out like that. It came out as garbled sounds, like talking under water.

"You're probably asking yourself where you are," a deep voice said. The face in front of her pulsed like some psychedelic image, then sharpened into focus.

She nodded. No use trying to talk. And even if she could articulate, her mouth was incredibly dry. Like nothing she'd ever experienced. Her tongue stuck to the roof of her mouth.

11

It was an acutely unpleasant sensation, like every other sensation she was feeling.

"Before I tell you where you are," that deep voice continued, "you are probably very thirsty and your head hurts."

Exactly. She nodded again.

He held up a bottle of pills. "This is ibuprofen. Notice that the bottle is new." He broke the seal, shook three tablets into the palm of his hand. His hand was very large and the tablets looked tiny in his palm. "Water. Brand new bottle." He held up a small water bottle, waggled it. Broke that seal and held it up.

"Open up." That deep voice held *command*. Elle wasn't used to a commanding voice, so when he brought the pills to her mouth, she opened up. "Swallow." Another command as he held the bottle to her mouth.

Oh, yes! Water! She was absolutely parched. He tipped the bottle at exactly the right angle so that she could drink without choking. She finished the small bottle and he put it down on a table next to his chair.

But ... why would she need help drinking? And ... her hands weren't working. She looked down in befuddlement and saw that her wrists were tied to the arms of the chair with a soft cloth. She rattled her hands, shaking her arms, but it was no use. She was ... tied up.

Elle blinked. Her mind wasn't working properly. She rarely drank, she never used drugs and her mind was what she was, so when it wasn't working, she was lost.

The man sitting across from her was studying her carefully, seeming to follow her thought processes. She didn't know him but she'd seen him —

All of a sudden, a surge of clarity shot through her. The clouds lifted and red-hot rage filled her head.

"You!" she said sharply.

"Me," he answered.

"At the —" she pulled a blank.

"Conference in Oxford. N-person Non-cooperative Strategy. Very interesting talk you gave, didn't understand a word."

"You — you accosted me afterward!"

He shook his head, expression gentle. "No, Elle. I didn't accost you. I don't use violence against women. But I did drug you."

And just like that, Elle realized the extreme danger she was in.

Icy terror flooded her veins. She was tied up, incapacitated. In a place she didn't recognize. She looked around, trying to figure out where she was. It was a luxurious apartment or hotel suite, with no personal touches at all. Neutral color palette, top-of-the-line furniture. She craned her neck to the right and saw a high-end kitchenette and three doors that were closed. Where was she? Was she even still in England?

She opened her mouth to scream and he shook

his head sharply.

"I wouldn't advise screaming. The ibuprofen will just be starting to kick in and screaming would make that headache worse." He shrugged a massive shoulder apologetically. "You don't know where we are. We're in a luxury apartment building in London, but that's all I can say for now. I'm sorry to have to tell you that this apartment has been soundproofed. And my company owns the apartments on either side. So if you scream, you'll only give yourself a headache and no one will come."

Oh, God. This was *terrifying*. She'd been kidnapped. Drugged and kidnapped and tied up. If that wasn't every woman's nightmare, she didn't know what was.

And though the man sitting across from her looked relaxed and almost smiling, he was huge. She remembered that when he stopped her in Oxford, she'd had to look up — way *way* up — at him. Even sitting down, she could see that he had enormous shoulders tapering down to a lean waist. He looked like an athlete. He looked like a man who knew how to use his body. And though he was dressed well — black sweater, fine black pants, shiny brand-new boots — his hands were rough. As if he used them a lot.

To strangle women?

No, don't think like that. She couldn't panic. She had to think her way out of this.

"Why —" Elle's voice gave out. She wanted so

badly to be nonchalant but terror closed her throat. "Why am I here? What do you want with me?"

Her voice shook.

Why was she here, a prisoner of this man? So he could rape her, strangle her, torture her? Leave her rotting body in this apartment where no one could hear her screams as she died?

"I hate that look," he said, frowning. "I'm not going to hurt you."

"So you say." She swallowed. That small bottle of water seemed like an hour ago. She wanted to ask for more water but didn't know if — if he'd let her go to the bathroom. Having to pee in her pants was too horrific a thought. She'd rather go thirsty.

"Yes." He nodded sharply. "I do."

Elle cocked her head, watching him carefully. She wasn't a keen observer of people. Mostly she lived inside her own head. So maybe she was way off base here. But … he didn't *seem* like a maniac or a torturer or rapist or murderer. Surely psychopaths gave off … vibes. Or something. Surely the agitation in their minds would be reflected in their bodies.

This man was utterly still and utterly relaxed. And though she had no idea if she was reading him right, she didn't get violent vibes from him.

Of course, the maids might find her headless body two days from now because Elle had no sense how to judge people, except for academically. Never in her life had she had to gauge whether someone might be a violent monster and strangle her to death.

"What's your name?" she blurted. And then immediately wondered — was that a smart thing to ask? Maybe if she knew his name and survived the ordeal, he'd kill her anyway because she knew who he was.

On the other hand, in the thrillers she'd read, kidnappees tried to establish a relationship with the kidnapper, the theory being that if he knew she liked her steak rare, that would humanize her and he'd be less eager to whack her.

She tensed her wrists. The cloths tying them were soft but well-knotted. But if she could ever get him to release her she could ... what? There was a very handsome brass lamp. Maybe she could grab it and brain him with it. On the marble-topped kitchen counter was a plate and a wine glass with some wine still in it. Could she rush to grab it, smash it on the counter and go for the jugular?

"My name is Bennett Cameron," he said easily. "And I'm an expert in close protection."

He was watching her very carefully and sighed at her blank look. "I'm a bodyguard."

Elle's mind stuttered. This was the last thing she was expecting. A bodyguard?

"Okay, now pay attention." He straightened a little, reached for something and Elle's heart jumped into her throat. But he was only reaching for a laptop. Which showed how terrified and drug-addled she was, because she usually noticed IT before she noticed people. "I'm going to show you something. Something that should reassure you. After which I will release you from your bonds and I would be very grateful if you didn't lunge for the brass lamp or the glass on the counter because believe me, I'm faster than you. And bigger and stronger, too, while we're at it. Now I know you're smarter than me, but we're in a very Darwinian situation right now, and your smarts aren't going to be very useful. Are we clear?"

Elle sat breathing for a moment, trying to sort out what he was telling her. He was saying that he'd show her something after which he'd let her go and she'd understand it was … what? All a big misunderstanding? She was here, in this strange room, tied up after he'd drugged her, but it wasn't the way it looked? On the other hand, he also told her not to try anything because he was bigger and faster than she was and he'd win.

It wasn't often that Elle found herself in a pissing contest with a man where the winning attribute was strength not intelligence. But this was one of those times and she didn't stand a chance against his muscle.

"Elle?"

She looked up at him, miserable.

He closed his eyes briefly and sighed. "Damn. Don't look at me like that. Come on, watch this and then we'll talk."

"And you'll release me from my bonds," she whispered.

"Yes. And then I'll release you from your bonds."

"Okay." Her mouth was dry. She had no idea

what kind of video he was going to show her. Maybe it was of some other victim? What had happened to them? Something so awful she'd relinquish all thoughts of fighting back? "Let's — let's see."

He put the laptop on his lap, turned it around so the screen faced her and pressed play.

"Hello darling." Elle's eyes opened wide. That was her father! Her father sitting on a chair she didn't recognize in a room she didn't recognize. He looked a thousand years old, paper white, with huge dark bags under his eyes. "There's a problem."

Bennett didn't watch the video, he watched her. He knew what the video said, he'd been listening via Skype when it was recorded, directing what was said. There was no information given in the video other than what was necessary to reassure Clifford Ricks's daughter. Bennett had made sure of that. Ricks had been sick with worry and though he was normally very tight-fisted with information — he basically sold information after all — he'd started blabbing. He'd given his location, his plans and basically painted a target on his back. Bennett had had him turn the video recording function off and start over, three times.

The end result was scary for a daughter, but there was nothing in it that Ricks's enemies could use.

As she listened to her father, Elle's face turned as white as his and her eyes grew impossibly huge. Her hands were shaking and her breathing was fast. She was a little shocky. But Bennett didn't try to reassure her. Long experience taught him that cocky principals got themselves into messes. He'd taken a bullet once for a principal who didn't take the danger seriously. The more frightened they were, the more they followed his orders and didn't take risks.

This was serious shit and she had to take it seriously.

It was a real pity that he had to scare this beautiful and super smart woman, but it was for her own good. The threat was real and the more deeply she understood that, the better her chances of survival.

"Honey," Ricks was saying, "I'm … having some difficulties."

Well, that was putting it mildly. He'd lost ten million dollars of the Russian Mafiya's money. Poof! Up in smoke.

But Clifford Ricks was a money man and to some degree he was therefore a bullshitter. The words 'I fucked up, badly' wouldn't leave his mouth. Couldn't. A lifetime of talking prospects up made him incapable of expressing the brutal truth.

"I have some very bad people hunting me and I'm afraid they are hunting you, too."

Bennett tapped a key that stopped the video, at a moment that made Ricks look almost insane. Everything in his face drooped—jowls, cheeks, mouth.

Usually freshly barbered, his face was covered in white scruff, his hair stuck out in white clumps, his eyebrows and nose hairs needed clipping. And he was dripping with perspiration, though Bennett knew that wherever Ricks was, it would be climate-controlled.

Ricks had spent a lifetime drowning in comfort. Possible impending death and possible torture of his only child wouldn't change that.

Bennett waited for Elle's eyes to turn to him. Her reflexes were slow. She was having trouble processing this. This was not an abstract math problem, this was life at its rawest.

Bennett hated this, just hated it. Fuck Ricks for plunging this brainy, beautiful young woman into his crazy mess that could turn violent at any moment.

"Elle?" He kept his voice low, gentle. Finally, her face turned toward him, eyes tracking a second later.

"Y-yes?"

"You have to pay attention to this part. It's important." She swallowed and jerked her head up and down.

"Focus, now," he said quietly. This to a woman who kept three dense pages of math formulae in her head. He'd seen it. She was nothing *but* focus, except for something like this, completely outside her wheelhouse.

He pressed a key and the video picked up where it had been stopped.

"I invested some money on behalf of ... some Russian gentlemen." *Yeah, gentlemen,* Bennett thought sourly. *Russian mob is more like it.* The Lipovs were no gentlemen. They were more like feral animals. "They had a considerable sum they wanted to invest and I saw a good deal in airlines and air transport."

"Airlines! Air transport!" She gasped, turned to Bennett.

He stopped the video.

"Yeah. This was two weeks before the two volcanos erupted." All air transport worldwide had been closed down for ten days, as two volcanos erupted within 24 hours of each other, spewing uncounted tons of ash into the air. One in Iceland, one in Hawaii. Airlines and air transport companies took a huge hit. Many had gone bankrupt.

Bennett turned the video back on.

Ricks huffed out a wheezing breath. "As you know, Elle, air transport of goods and passengers came to a grinding halt," Ricks said on the screen. "And there were huge secondary effects on the market. The Dow Jones lost two thousand points, the Nasdaq lost a third of its value and the FTS and the Nikkei lost half theirs."

"That's a lot of money," Bennett said while they listened to Ricks wheezing on the video.

She shot him a *No shit, Sherlock* look.

"I lost something like eight hundred million dollars in a few days." Ricks wiped sweat out of his eyes. "With a — with a normal, institutional investor, I could explain. I *have* explained it to most of my clients. I've taken a big hit but it's force majeure. An act of God. And I can make that money back for them during the course of a year. Maybe two, at the most. But these people ..." His face trembled, jowls shaking. "These people are totally unreasonable."

Elle nodded to Bennett to stop the recording and turned to him. "Who are they, these investors?"

Bennett's jaw clenched. *Your father's amazing greed got away from him and he accepted money from the worst people on earth. What the fuck was he thinking?* But he couldn't say that. It wouldn't help anyone. However, much as he didn't want to bad-mouth Ricks in front of his daughter, she had to understand the danger she was in. He said what he could.

"I suspect that he didn't recognize the investors for what they were. Front men for the Russian Mafiya." He looked her straight in her intensely blue eyes. "They are very bad people."

Her face was frozen. She nodded and he pressed play again.

"Today they shot the head of my accounting department." Ricks swallowed heavily. Bennett had been a little surprised when Ricks said that for the video. What he didn't tell his daughter was that Ford Atkins, his CFO, had been taken to a field in New Jersey and staked out. As a camera recorded every little detail, an off-camera gun shot out Atkins' kneecaps, shot his hands and his elbows. The camera was unwavering in its focus while Atkins took two hours to die. "They want their money back or they will —" he stopped, sweat pouring off him. "They will hurt you," he continued hoarsely. "And they will hurt me."

The mobsters wouldn't kill Ricks because he was their only hope of getting their money back, but they could and were making his life hell. But if they got their hands on Elle, they would definitely hurt her. And send Ricks the video in 4K hi-def.

They didn't fuck around.

Ricks was lucky he was in Paris when the threat came, Elle was in Oxford and Bennett was at his company's headquarters in London. Made things easier. If Elle had been in Boston, Bennett wouldn't have made it to her in time. She could be screaming in agony this very minute if fate hadn't made them all geographically close.

Ricks swallowed heavily, the wattles in his neck quivering. "I called in a company we've been doing business with for a long time. I've asked the head of the company, Bennett Cameron —" here Ricks clicked something off screen and an old photo of Bennett appeared. It was taken from his company's website which was very spare with information. "So when this man comes for you, go with him, honey. I am being protected by my men but I insisted that Bennett himself protect you. I also insisted that he not tell me where he is taking you. I have no idea where you are, but I know you'll be safe with him."

The camera of his laptop stayed on his face for a full minute as he sat and breathed heavily and sweated. Finally, in a corner of the screen, his mottled, shaking hand reached out and the camera winked off.

There was dead silence. Bennett let her work her way through this. Elle Castle was a highly intelligent young woman but this must have seemed like a message from another planet to her.

Unfortunately, it wasn't another planet, it was this one, planet Earth. A deadly, violent place where people did awful things. Always had. Always would.

She went deep inside herself for a couple of minutes. Her eyes were unfocused and she was completely still. When she looked up at him again, he spoke.

"We good? You're not going to try to bash my head in or bite me or break a glass on my face?"

"We're good." Her voice was calm. Bennett had to admire her. She was shocked and frightened and probably still a little afraid of him — though he'd done his best to make sure she understood he meant her no harm — but she kept her dignity. She lifted her wrists a little off the arms of the chair. He'd deliberately left the restraints a little loose. Anyone else and he'd have tied them with plasticuffs so tightly they'd cut off circulation. But not her. She just needed to be immobilized until he could show her the video and explain. She lifted her wrists again. "Can you cut me loose?"

"Of course." Bennett reached down to his boot and slid out his sweet little Gerber Mark 2, which he kept razor sharp. Before she even had a chance to wince, he'd sliced through the cloth and freed her.

He hadn't looked at her wrists while doing it — he had excellent peripheral vision — but watched her eyes.

In combat, you watched the eyes.

If by any chance she was thinking of escaping, this would be the moment. He was ready to block any movement, though he hated the idea of hurting her in any way.

He spared an angry thought for her fucking dad, though, whose greed had put her in this position. Where she had to be kidnapped to save her from violent monsters. What dad would do that?

Nothing showed on his face, though. Nothing ever showed on Bennett's face that he didn't want there.

The instant her wrists were free, Bennett lifted his hands and sat back. There was nothing she could hurt him with within reach, but if she wanted to slap him, he'd just take it. He'd taken worse.

But she didn't slap him. She merely sat quietly, rubbing her wrists, watching him. "We good?" he asked again.

She nodded, that shiny blue-black mass of hair sliding forward then shifting back. He had a sudden urge to touch her hair, just to see if it was as cool as it looked. It looked like midnight on a moonless night. And, since he was thinking about forbidden gestures, he'd like to outline that gorgeous face with a fingertip, and trace the contours of her mouth. It was the kind actresses went to a plastic surgeon for, only hers was 100% natural. Lips pillowy, soft, with a little crease in the bottom lip.

A mouth made for kissing.

Whoa.

This was a *principal,* for fuck's sake. A client. Or rather, her father was the client, but still. Bennett never had any trouble at all keeping his personal feelings separate from the job, but this woman pushed all his buttons.

Super smart and competent, right now she was looking lost and scared and, well, lonely. And he'd been the one to do that to her.

Fuck Ricks, he thought for the billionth time.

"So, I have a few service announcements," he said.

"Okay." She cocked her head and directed that amazing gaze at him, listening carefully.

"First of all, we're going to be here a while, so there are some arrangements to be made."

She blinked. "How long?"

Bennett shrugged. "I have no idea. Quite literally. This lasts until your father says his problems are over." And God knew when that would be. The guy had to make up a shortfall of ten million dollars when he'd probably lost a billion or two between his own money and his clients' money. Even for a financial genius, that had to take time.

She exhaled. "What if it takes months? Years?"

"Then we'll be here months. Years." Though Bennett didn't think it would take that long. Ricks would die of a heart attack if nothing else. "There's nothing you or I can do about that. And if you're thinking of eventually running away, I wouldn't if I were you." He hesitated a moment, then let her have it. "These guys want leverage over your father, want it in the worst way. I guess they think he's holding out on them and that if they had you as a hostage, he would just hand over what he owes them. The thing is —these people are ruthless. I'm sure your father had no idea who they really were when he accepted the contract. Mobsters tend to use more civilized front men so your father wouldn't have known how brutal the guys with the money are."

She leaned forward a little. "If they're so brutal, then surely they will go after my father? Grab him, try to squeeze him."

Bennett nodded sharply. "Good thinking, only you're missing some information."

She gave a half smile. "I'm sure I'm missing a lot of information. I know nothing of my father's business. Just as I know nothing of his life."

It occurred to Bennett how stupid Ricks was. Not only in keeping a woman like Elle, a woman any father would be incredibly proud of, out of his life, but also by not inviting her into his business. A genius-level daughter steeped in math would be a hedge fund owner's dream.

But Clifford Ricks was one of those men who were money smart and life stupid.

"Your father is being protected by his men. And

like you, he's in hiding. He's waving his magic money wand in some cave somewhere —" though knowing Ricks, he'd have insisted on every possible luxury, "waiting this thing out."

Bennett's money was on Paris.

"So — you mentioned arrangements?" She put her hands — slim and elegant — on the arms of her chair but stopped and looked at him. "May I stand up?"

"God yes." Bennett stood up, gave her his hand. She'd probably be stiff and sore. "Except for leaving this apartment, there's not much you can't do. I'm sorry if you feel like a prisoner. I'm just trying to keep you safe."

She took his hand and there was some crazy shit. Like an electrical crackle, like a transfer of energy. They both withdrew their hands and she looked at him, startled.

Well, *hell*.

That was sexual energy, off the scale. From a woman he was forbidden from touching as long as he was under contract to protect her.

Fuck.

It was going to be a long job.

Three

Elle snatched her hand away from his. The touch of his hand to hers had *burned.* Well, not burned actually, it was more like an electric shock. He must have felt it too because his hand dropped. They stared at each other. She was sure her face showed consternation. His showed nothing at all, but then if he was in security, he'd probably honed that expressionless face to perfection. She didn't need a poker face in her job, and she could feel the shocked expression she had.

They stood there like dummies. Someone had to break the ice. "So," she said, turning away, trying to coax her face into bland lines, "what kind of arrangements?"

He was fast on the uptake, but then someone who was expected to leap in front of a bullet couldn't be slow. Or was that only for Secret Service agents protecting the president?

No, this guy looked like he'd leap in front of a bullet. Maybe catch it in his teeth, spit it back out.

Instead of answering, he turned his computer toward them and brought up a page. Amazon, she saw to her surprise. He was going to order a book?

"You're going to need ... things." He waved his hand at her and looked — was that possible? — a little embarrassed. There was a tiny little smear of red along his cheekbones, looking odd on that hard face.

Well, this was amusing. Did Mr. Super Tough Guy get all embarrassed at the idea that she would eventually need tampons, or was he talking toothbrush and toothpaste? "Things?" she repeated, arching a brow.

"Things." He entered some data. "Clothes first of all. That jacket of yours, for instance. Is it a designer thing?"

His mind seemed to leap from subject to subject. She looked down at herself. She loved this jacket, with its off-center cut. "Well, yes. It's a Vivienne Westwood. Why?"

"It looks nice on you, really nice. I've never heard of Vivienne Westwood but I take it she's well known?"

Elle nodded. Where was he going with this?

"So you're on a credit card with unlimited credit. It's a genuine card but a fake person and the delivery address is to a courier service who will get the stuff to us fast. Order from any online shop you want. Use the card to buy as many clothes and ... things as you like but they should be bland. Or at least not your usual style and not the usual designers you choose."

She nodded again. "No personal patterns that could be followed, correct?"

His mouth quirked, as much emotion as he'd allow himself. "Correct. Buy whatever you want in whatever quantity. Clothes, shoes, underwear, lingerie, ah … creams and makeup. Everything that would be in your suitcase for at least a month's stay in a hotel. From the skin out. Mainly indoor wear, we won't be going out, certainly not outside this complex. Buy some exercise kind of stuff, one of the rooms has been set up as a gym."

Elle didn't do gyms, not even the fancy ones, "This complex? Does it have a pool? I'll buy several swimsuits." She did do pools. She swam every day.

"There's a pool." Bennett shifted in his seat as if he were uncomfortable. "There are security cameras everywhere in this complex. We'll have to see —"

"I've got an idea about that. A little program I've written. It should mask my presence."

A corner of his mouth lifted. "Well that would be useful. So yeah, buy yourself as many swim suits as you need. Nothing too showy."

Elle refrained from rolling her eyes. "I promise not to buy those bikinis that are basically dental floss. I usually use racing suits anyway. Don't worry."

He slid a glossy menu in front of her. "While you're ordering a wardrobe online, I'll order up dinner." His finger found something. "They have a —" He squinted, "quinoa, beetroot and avocado salad. Sounds good. Do you want that?"

Ack. It sounded awful. Elle read through the rest of the menu. "Certainly not. I want the 8 oz filet mignon burger, rare, chili fries and the chocolate cheesecake. It's bad enough being kidnapped, my life taken away from me. The least you can do is feed me properly."

"Yes, ma'am. We can definitely do that." He grinned, teeth very white in his tanned face. And oh, God, he shouldn't do that. Grin. He was attractive in a scary and off-putting kind of way when he was drugging her and kidnapping her. He looked tough and completely charmless. But if now he was going to turn on the charm …

"I need to take a shower," she said, standing up abruptly. "Then I'll order clothes and things. They'll be delivered tomorrow morning?"

"Some things might arrive this evening. Go ahead and take your shower. You'll find a tee shirt that will cover you. There'll be a couple of clean pairs of yoga pants one of our female operatives left in one of the cupboards. They might fit, though she's taller than you. By the time you finish your shower and finish ordering whatever you need, dinner should be here."

Elle escaped into the bathroom because his deep voice was creating weird vibrations in her stomach. No doubt an effect of the drug.

The bathroom was sumptuous, even more sumptuous than that of the hotel in Moscow at her last conference. It didn't have rose-scented water but it had everything else. Elle switched the setting of the shower to high, just below lobster-cooking-in-boiling-water, and stood beneath the huge shower head. Water always revived her. Maybe she'd been a mermaid in a previous life. She'd had two major insights while swimming. If nothing else, flowing water calmed her.

She needed calming.

She was stuck for the foreseeable future with an attractive man who had excellent manners if you could overlook drugging her and tying her up.

The thing was, he'd made it clear that within the confines of the apartment she could do as she pleased. But her autonomy ended at the door. Beyond that door, she was essentially a prisoner. In a deluxe prison, it was true, but a prisoner nonetheless.

Usually Elle could think her way out of any dilemma, but not this one. Even if she could outsmart Bennett, which was not a given, her father was in danger and she couldn't do anything to worsen his situation.

Not to mention the fact that she didn't want to be grabbed off the streets by Russian mobsters and tortured. Nope.

She switched the water off and grabbed a towel. Damn. She couldn't even complain about the towels. This one was blindingly white and super fluffy. And, sure enough, there was a brand-new huge tee that was essentially a dress on her. She looked down. Yes, it hit the top of her knees. She'd had sun dresses that showed a lot more. Because with a guy like Bennett who exuded testosterone from every pore, it was going to be necessary to stay off his sexual radar. Not that she was worried he'd force himself on her. He'd made that clear.

No, the problem was her. He was … attractive. Hot, actually. It had been a long time since Elle had found any man attractive. Most of her dealings with men were with male mathematicians, most of them belonging to what she called, in the deepest recesses of her mind, The Dandruff Brigade. In her dealings with colleagues, not one hormone was involved, just her neurons. Being with Bennett she'd felt hormones wake up that had been napping for a long time.

This was going to be difficult and awkward if she couldn't keep a tight hold on herself.

She held up the yoga pants. The woman they belonged to must have been a giant. The soft top had to be pulled up practically under her armpits and she had to roll the pant legs up a couple of times. She looked like a child dressed up in her parents' clothes. No. She pulled the yoga pants down and off and checked herself in the mirror, wearing only the giant tee. Tomorrow more clothes would be arriving. For the moment, this would have to do. The tee was excellent quality cotton, came almost down to her knees and was completely modest. No one could tell she was naked underneath.

She opened the bathroom door and walked out.

Oh fuck. Fuck fuck *fuck*.

She was naked underneath his tee shirt. She hadn't put on the yoga pants, either. Well, Charlie was a strapping woman, over six feet tall and heavily muscled. Elle was about 5' 4" and slender, almost delicate. But not putting on the pants … Jesus.

Did she have a clue?

The opening of his tee was so large on her he could see delicate collar bones and the collar tended to slip over one shoulder. Her slender legs were outlined. And she wasn't wearing a bra. Was she wearing panties?

The fuck was *wrong* with him?

He shouldn't care if his principals were buck naked. The only thing he ever cared about was handing them back when the danger was over in the same shape they'd been in when entrusted into his care. Without even a nick or a dent.

Unfortunately, Bennett knew exactly what she felt like. In Oxford, he'd basically held her up as they maneuvered to the car he had waiting and then he'd half carried her to the helo, then he'd had to jab her again once they landed in London so that she was pliant as they went from the helo to the BMW waiting on the tarmac, down to the underground garage in Sparrow Square then up the back elevator. That second jab had been a stronger dose.

Bennett had very carefully not felt her up. That would have been creepy. But he'd have had to have been dead not to notice the slender curves, that strong lithe body. And he'd have had to have been dead not to be a little aroused.

All right, watching her coming out of the bathroom with a puff of steam coming from the shower behind her, a lot aroused.

Shit.

He was behind the island, which hit him at waist level, and he had to stay that way. She was walking toward him, cobalt-blue eyes fixed on him, and it was as if she could read his mind. It was not a pleasant feeling.

He grabbed a stemmed glass, uncorked a good red and poured her a generous measure. He slid it across the marble counter of the island. "Here. Have a glass of wine while you order what you need."

She nodded, picking up the glass. Thank God she sat in profile to him. She sipped and sat, clicking on a key. He could tell the monitor came to life by the reflection off her pale skin. "Do you have the parameters of what you can order?"

She was scrolling. "I think so. No Vivienne Westwood, no Stella McCartney, no quirky modern designers. Bland things that won't make me stand out."

He let out a little sigh of relief. "Exactly. Get everything you could possibly need, clothes or not. And remember, no limits on the budget."

She was studying the screen and her mouth lifted in a half smile. "I imagine most women would kill to hear that."

"Dream come true."

Elle sighed. "Not really. I hate shopping. I order everything online anyway. So — here goes." She bent forward a little and disappeared into the monitor.

Whew. That weird energy that sprang up between them flipped off like a light switch when she turned her attention to other things. It was a little scary when she focused on him. Scary and arousing.

Damn.

Bennett rummaged in the cabinets above the sink. He hadn't been in this apartment for a couple of years, but … yup. Everything was still well organized. Plates where plates should be. Glasses where glasses should be. Cutlery in the drawer. Place mats below.

No food, though, just wine. Not even staples. They could eat take-out meals for a long time. Sparrow Square boasted a bistrot, a café, a brasserie and a full-service restaurant and they all delivered to the apartments in the complex.

But Bennett was a good cook and he had to do something while they were confined to the apartment. There were plenty of shops in the area. He could order staples and groceries from …

"Done," she said crisply from behind him.

He turned in surprise. "Done?"

"Yes. I told you I hate shopping but I know what I like, so I got it done fast."

Not ten minutes had passed. "I, um, don't want to question the speed of your shopping skills, but we might have to be here for a while so …"

"Ten sets of pajamas. Ten yoga outfits, top and bottom. Ten sweat suits. Ten sets of underwear. Ten silk camisoles. Twenty pairs of socks. Ten sweaters, five cashmere, five cotton and silk. Ten shirts, five silk, five linen. Ten pairs of pants, wool and cotton. Two raincoats. Three wool jackets. Five swimsuits—I really hope to get some swimming in. Four ballerina slippers for inside the apartment. Two pairs of boots. Four cashmere shawls. A down coat. Toiletries. A small " She rattled everything off as if reading from the monitor, though she'd closed her laptop. "And a partridge in a pear tree. I should be okay for a while. I spent five thousand pounds."

Bennett shrugged. Didn't make any difference what she spent, it was all going on the bill anyway. He wished she'd spent more so her father would think twice about investing for the Russian Mob. But what was done was done.

"That's, uh, great. Just … great. We should be … great." Damn it! Why was his tongue stuck in great mode?

The doorbell rang and he checked the monitor on the corner of the kitchen cabinet. There was another one in the living room and one in each of the two bedrooms. A waiter stood outside patiently, slightly distorted because of the fish-eye lens that showed that no one stood to one side. One waiter, alone, with a food cart. The waiter was wafer-thin and there was no possible weapon that wouldn't show beneath his skin-tight uniform. He looked about twelve, weighed about 120 lbs and had pimples.

This wasn't a mobster.

But Bennett made a note to ask for updated photos of every single server in the complex, even part-time staff. He'd upload all the photos into his facial recog system.

But in the meantime …

He stood in the doorway, blocking any view of the room, though Elle wasn't visible from the door.

"Thank you," he said in his best English accent. No sense the waiter knowing there was an American in the room. He held out a tenner between two fingers and it disappeared instantly.

Bennett was also gratified to see that the waiter didn't look twelve years old in close up. He looked ten. There was another monitor beside the door and Bennett watched him walk away with a smile, holding the tenner.

Bennett wheeled the cart toward the dining table, surprised to see that Elle had put away her laptop and had set the table already with place mats and glasses.

Man, that woman was fast. He liked that.

"Smells delicious." She had her straight, pretty nose right over the covered dishes and inhaled.

"It does." Bennett waved a hand at her chair. "Please take a —"

But she was already seated, napkin on her lap, and was looking up expectantly.

Oh man. She was just so pretty. But beyond the good looks there was this vibrant air about her, like a humming bird, as if she operated at a higher frequency than other people. It made him feel good, just sitting across from her.

She attacked her hamburger as if she were starving. She probably was. A lot had happened since she'd finished her speech in Oxford, none of it involving food. She'd been drugged, kidnapped, flown to London, woken up, absorbed the fact that her father was under attack and that she'd been put under a dome just like her hamburger.

"So." She swallowed a bite of the hamburger. She ate very neatly but fast. Half of it was gone and he wondered if he should share part of his huge steak and mango salad with her. She waved a finger between them. "How does this work?"

"This?" Bennett realized that being with her meant that he'd have to operate at a higher frequency too.

Elle huffed out an impatient breath. "This bodyguarding thing. How does it work?"

He tasted his salad. It was excellent. He was sure he could reproduce it. "Well," he answered, "it's a lot less complex than game theory. Basically, I stick close to you and form a barrier around you. That's more or less it. There are theories about bodyguarding, lines of fire, perimeters of protection, but that's the essence. Sticking close by the client — called the principal in the trade — and forming a barrier of protection."

"Huh." He could practically see her head buzzing.

"So — you'd take a bullet for me?"

He put his fork down and leaned forward. "Yes. Absolutely." His voice was dead serious because he was. "That's the job."

Those bright deep blue eyes widened. "And have you? Taken a bullet."

"Yes." He didn't particularly want to talk about it. "I have." Several, in fact.

"Have you lost anyone?"

"No." His voice was curt and he didn't want to be curt with her. "To tell you the truth, I don't do close protection work much any more and we're moving into other areas of security anyway. I'm the head of my company and we're growing fast. It's a dangerous world. Running the company takes up most of my time. I only accepted this job because your father insisted."

"Well." He'd give a lot of money to be able to decipher the thoughts buzzing around in her head. She smiled. "I'm glad you did."

He smiled back. "Yeah. So am I."

Four

Being kidnapped was exhausting. Luckily Elle was in the right bed for it.

The bed was insanely comfortable, the sheets smelled of lavender, the dinner she'd had sat warmly in her stomach and, it must be said, she had a very efficient guard dog right next door.

Bennett had offered to sleep on the couch if it made her feel better, but he'd also walked her through the safety features of the apartment, which were amazing. After the tour, she'd insisted that he take the other bedroom.

The apartment made Fort Knox look like amateur hour.

The windows looked out over a very pretty internal courtyard and the panes had been replaced with bullet-resistant glass and a film that let in light but made the apartment invisible from the outside. The front door was essentially a vault and had hydraulics fitted to make it easier to open and close.

Most luxury apartments had smoke detectors and this one did too, of course. It could also detect most biological and radiological weapons. Monitors showed every inch of the corridor outside.

So she was going to be super safe, but without anything to do.

That was going to be hard. Elle was used to being busy. She was a visiting professor on two campuses on the East Coast and she traveled constantly giving talks. True, she was writing a book on Stochastic Theories in Game Playing, but there were only so many hours in a day you could write.

Had her father pushed the panic button unnecessarily? Calling in the Marines? Or whatever branch of the military Bennett came from. Because clearly he'd been military at some point in his life, with that ramrod-straight posture, that no-nonsense air.

He was a fascinating man, her bodyguard. It wasn't just a question of his … physical charms, though they were pretty potent. Elle didn't really frequent physically powerful men, so she was open to the idea that maybe she was blinded by muscles.

Could be.

He sure had a lot of them.

Elle could almost feel her brain retreating back from the neocortex, site of abstract thought, to the hypothalamus, site of basic instincts. Somewhere in the distant past, a great-great-a thousand times great-grandmother of hers had chosen a mate specifically for his physique, to keep her from harm.

And thousands of years later, her brainy great-great-a thousand times great-granddaughter, who thought herself well above that sort of thing, was falling into a prehistoric trap.

But it wasn't just muscles or the eye candy thing. She could go to the beach for that. No, he seemed to be on the ball, really intelligent in a street-smarts kind of way. She traveled a lot and considered herself savvy but he'd kidnapped her in plain sight and secreted her away without breaking a sweat. Maybe he'd done that sort of thing before, but it had been done very smoothly.

And though he hadn't discussed his company at all, she'd googled it, after asking its name. BMC Security. After his name, Bennett Cameron. There was a middle name there. M. Michael? Morris?

Manly.

The company website was amazing. Snazzy and cool, giving away very little information but what there was clearly got across the message that if you had a problem, they'd take care of it for you. No rates sheet. If you had to ask, you couldn't afford it. Very slickly done.

No photographs of employees, just Bennett's photo. He'd told her the company employed 150 people, but they remained anonymous. There was no phone number to call. Just an email. In a tiny font.

That photograph of Bennett ... not a vanity shot. It wasn't posed and the few wrinkles on his face — more a product of the sun than age — hadn't been photoshopped out. But his vitality leaped off the page.

When she closed her eyes she could see his face

behind her lids. Serious, without being pompous, good bone structure, and those penetrating eyes that seemed to see everything.

Too revved by the events of the day, she turned over in bed. She wasn't going to get any sleep at all, she thought, as she lay on the extraordinarily comfortable bed, with its memory foam mattress and billion-thread count sheets.

She was asleep a second later.

After a few minutes, she opened her eyes, fully refreshed. *That was quick*, she thought. Then checked her watch. It was 9 am and she'd slept for eleven hours straight. Strange what being kidnapped could do. Normally she was a very light sleeper.

Maybe it was the silence in the room, the silence of solid walls and tapestry that soaked up sound. They were in the heart of an apartment complex and not a sound.

Wait — there was a slight ... thumping. Like a heartbeat. A fast heartbeat. A fluttering sound.

She threw back the duvet and walked barefoot around the apartment. Was she alone? Wasn't Bennett supposed to stick by her side? He wasn't in the other bedroom. The door was open and she could see inside. The room was a replica of hers, only the walls were forest green, the carpet and duvet steel gray. The ensuite-bathroom door was open and the bathroom was empty. Not in the kitchen or the living room. That left one room and sure enough that odd fluttering sound became stronger as she walked toward it.

She opened the door, stopped on the threshold and stared. The fluttering sound was much louder. Bennett, in a sweat-soaked gray wife beater, running shorts and bandages around his hands, was beating a cylindrical bag to death. His movements were steady and brutal and the bag swung from the ceiling, making arcs as he beat it.

It was called a heavy bag and what he was doing looked simple but was anything but. Elle had tried it once, on a lark in a gym a fellow math nerd frequented, in a vain attempt to achieve muscle definition.

She'd been given gloves and a funny kind of leather helmet and had given the bag a heavy punch. It didn't move one inch. She gave it a heavier punch, one she felt to her toes, and it barely moved. Another and another and another. When she realized that this stupid bag was defeating her, she'd set her feet, really angry, and let go with a huge punch and the bag knocked her out on its return.

So watching Bennett in his workout routine, dancing with grace around the bag, landing blows that moved the bag back and forth, she knew that what he was doing required not only huge strength but fast reflexes.

She settled her shoulder against the doorjamb and watched, fascinated. Those muscles had been sort of hidden under his elegant clothes but now she could see that his body was almost brutal in its strength, though lean. He moved with power and grace, almost like an automaton, stepping lightly on his feet as if in a ballet.

His gaze met hers for one powerful second and she felt as if she'd been touched. No, not touched — *punched*. He focused again on the heavy bag but just that one glance made the skin over her entire body prickle, made her knees weak, made heat rush through her.

What she'd seen so far had been a tough guy — yeah. Sure. His entire job was being a tough guy. But also someone very civilized and polite, well-spoken, with excellent manners.

This man was an animal. A beast in its prime, beating on a heavy bag, leaving no doubt that he'd beat a bad guy the same way. Ruthlessly and efficiently. Every move he made was minimalist, no wasted energy, pure power.

Every muscle was in play from his shoulders to his calves. Long lean tight muscles. She'd never seen anything as beautiful as this and couldn't tear her eyes away.

Elle had no idea how much time passed as she watched him beat away at the heavy bag, unflagging and almost mechanical. It looked like he wasn't tiring. Would never tire.

She had been absolutely exhausted after just a minute or two trying to punch the heavy bag, getting nowhere. What he was doing was a feat of human strength and agility and, except for the copious sweat streaming off his body, he made it look easy.

She watched while the bag fluttered in such even rhythms it could have been a metronome. Finally, he stopped. Not because he was tired, but because some internal clock told him it was time. He stood, put out a bandaged hand to stop the heavy bag and looked over at her. He wasn't even breathing hard.

"Hi," he said. "Good morning. I hope you slept well. I need to take a shower, but breakfast is waiting. Your packages have arrived. I put them in the hallway closet."

Elle nodded, struck dumb. She simply stood, hand out, holding onto the door jamb for balance. He'd stopped sparring but that animal aura of strength and power was still there, almost visible. Not her civilized bodyguard but a man of immense power. And, unfortunately, a man who turned her on, massively.

Elle wasn't used to this. It floored her. She was used to being mildly attracted to men at times, usually mathematicians. The odd physicist. It was a pleasant feeling, like enjoying good music or a decent glass of wine. Not … this.

This was powerful, ran through her in surges like waves in the ocean, almost uncontrollable. She had to *think* to get her mouth to work, to get her feet moving.

"Yeah." She breathed in and out. "I'll … I'll see you for breakfast in a few minutes." And fled.

The packages were in the big hallway closet. There were a lot of them and she was happy with her choices. A complete wardrobe for being kidnapped and kept under wraps, everything perfect. She opened everything in her bedroom and put on a dark green cashmere sweater, black yoga pants and black ballerina slippers.

When she opened the bedroom door, the smell of breakfast assailed her and she realized how hungry she was.

"Hi." Bennett looked up from setting the table. "I heated everything up. I'm going to order some groceries in so we're not so dependent on take-out."

The table was properly set, with jugs of coffee, milk, a plate of scrambled eggs, five-grain bread, croissants, butter, a selection of jams and six pots of yogurt.

She sat down. "You cook?"

He grinned. "You bet. I like my food and eating out isn't always feasible. Not to mention eating out all the time isn't healthy."

Wow. He had reverted right back to being Civilized Affable Guy, dressed in a black turtle neck and black jeans. Looking perfectly normal, pulling out her chair and waiting until she sat down before sitting down himself.

But it was too late. She'd seen him in his Brutal

Pre-Modern Guy state and her hormones would never be the same.

Elle sat, gently unfolded the linen napkin and placed it over her lap, familiar movements that masked the slight trembling of her hands. Oh man. She wasn't used to having her brain go one way and her body another way entirely.

Her brain was handling a perfectly normal scenario. A meal with an attractive man, maybe some mild flirtation amongst the jams and yogurts. Paying some attention to the guy but also thinking about the day ahead.

That was her head.

Her body…damn.

Her body was on an entirely different page. Her body was at this very moment getting up and slithering onto his lap, winding her arms around his neck and kissing him. Not a nice peck on the lips, either. The kind of kiss she never indulged in but which she guessed he specialized in. The kind where you meld with the guy.

So here she was, completely split.

He leaned forward a little, frowning. "You okay?"

No, I'm not okay. I seem to have a compulsion to have sex with you because I saw you hitting a heavy bag, sweating, all your muscles on show.

This is highly unusual for me.

This was insane. She willed her hands to stop trembling and put on a polite smile. "Yes, I'm fine. Why do you ask?"

His face cleared. "For a second there … did you sleep all right? The bed is brand new and should be comfortable. I had memory foam mattresses put in."

She smiled a little at that thought. Primitive beserker with muscles up the wazoo, pondering memory foam mattresses. Did he also personally check the thread count of the sheets? The image of that calmed her down a little.

"Very comfortable, thank you. I slept like a log. I woke up with a slight headache, though."

He put his fork down and this time scowled. "Damn it. I was absolutely assured that the tranquilizer didn't have any long-term side effects." He reached out and placed his big hand over hers. "I am so sorry. If I'd had any choice in the matter … but I didn't. Your father made it clear that we had to act fast and I couldn't figure out any other way."

Their hands made such a sexy contrast. His was large, clean, nails manicured, but rough. She could feel the calluses against the back of her hand. Her own hand was soft. But then Elle didn't do much with her hands other than enter in data on a keyboard. Even their skin tones were sexy. His skin was tanned, that of a man who spent a lot of time outdoors. She didn't do well in the sun and was slathered with SPF 1000 whenever she went out.

Male. Female.

God. It hadn't really occurred to her how different the two genders were. To her, men were essentially women with extra meat dangling between their legs. Not this man. This man was Other.

"I don't think it's that," she said, leaving her hand where it was. "And the bed was super comfortable. But I'm worried about my father."

His hand briefly squeezed hers then he poured her a cup of coffee, put a croissant on her plate. His face turned serious. "I know the men protecting him. Nothing will happen to your father under their watch. Just like nothing will happen to you. He and you are perfectly safe."

Perfectly safe. It was an odd notion and not quite true. All sort of things could happen, some were even statistically probable. Her father was old and not in good health. He was diabetic and had four stents. He ate extremely badly and worked way too hard. He could drop dead of a heart attack at any moment. One had to stretch the odds for her because she was young and in perfect health. But there was terrorism and catastrophic storms and a recurrence of the Spanish Flu.

Zombies.

The sun could go nova.

"Have you lost anyone?"

He looked to one side and his jaw muscles clenched. "Not in this business, no." his voice was curt.

She cocked her head. "Did you lose someone when you were in the military?"

His own head whipped up. "How did you know I was in the military?"

"Laws of probability. You have skills that would be hard to gain in civilian life. You said you hadn't lost anyone in your business, so one infers that you lost someone in another business. Not too many businesses where you can lose people. Medicine, law enforcement and the military. That's about it."

"You're right. I'd say that was a good guess, but there probably wasn't any guesswork. The computer in your head put in the variables and came up with the correct answer."

That was exactly the way it was, but said like that, it made her sound like a … a robot. A machine.

Her gaze fell to her plate. Her appetite had suddenly deserted her. She followed the form of a small bird painted on the plate. Now that she noticed, that same small bird, stylized, very elegant, was embroidered in the tablecloth

"How do you want to spend your day?" Bennett asked. "I can't let you go out, but other than that, I can order in anything you like. Any books or movies. Any special foods. Anything you want."

The sleek stylized bird was replicated as a tiny icon on the handles of the silverware and one of the lamps had a brass base with the bird etched on it.

It all clicked.

"I know where we are!" she exclaimed. "We're in Sparrow Square!"

Bennett nodded. "Yeah. I'm sorry, I didn't mean to hide where we were. I didn't know whether you'd be familiar with the place."

The quiet stylish deluxe feel, the services on call … the birds. Sparrow Square. A full city block of deluxe apartments in the center of London, originally an Art Deco masterpiece, though the apartments had been renovated many times over the years. She'd always wanted to see it. Not necessarily as a deluxe prisoner, though.

"I've read a few articles on Sparrow Square. I also read that there is an Art Deco pool. I'd love to take a swim. Swimming is my stress relief."

Bennett cocked his head at the room where he'd been sparring with a bag. "We have a lot of weight machines, a stationary bike, you name it in there. If there's another piece of gym machinery you'd like …"

But she was already shaking her head. "If I'm forbidden to go to the pool, I can spend five minutes on the stationary bike, but I'd really rather go to the pool."

He sat looking at her, face completely expressionless. Elle understood very well that he was weighing pros and cons. Con: probably any outing outside of this apartment was not in the protocol, was verboten. Who knew who would be at the pool? Pro: she didn't know and he didn't know how long this situation would last. A week, a month, a year? *Years?* It was completely open ended. Just hunkering down in an apartment would drive anyone stir crazy. Elle was a homebody and enjoyed being at home, but there was a limit.

"There are risks," he said finally. "Staying here is more or less risk free, unless you post I AM HERE with a big red arrow on your Facebook page." He peered at her suspiciously. "That would be really dumb."

"It would be," she agreed. "Luckily, I don't have a Facebook page. I don't particularly like social media. It's too fragmented."

"Good. Makes things easier. Yogurt?" He pushed a pot of creamy yogurt over to her side of the table. He was stalling.

She just looked at him, waiting.

"I don't like it." He clenched his jaws. "I know you're safe here."

Elle leaned forward, pushing her plate out of the way. "You're worried about the in-house security recording, right?"

He nodded. "Yeah." The word sounded like it was pulled from his mouth with pliers.

"I have an idea, a way around that issue. If you're satisfied it's safe, I can go swimming. What do you say?"

He just looked at her, head to one side. He waited. She waited. Finally, he nodded his head. "Let's hear it."

"Even better, I'll show you."

Elle kept her face bland but inside she pulled a fist pump. Grabbing her cup of coffee, she went to her laptop. He looked at it curiously. It didn't have a brand logo and was gunmetal gray and left all other computers in the world in the dust.

Her baby.

She sat in front of the monitor and took a picture of herself, full face and in profile, left and right, entered the data and let her little program work its magic. Glancing up at him, she said, "I imagine you have access to the security cameras in the building, am I correct?"

A man like this, running a company like his, would not let the building guards run the security without oversight.

He hesitated and she waited patiently. Probably hacking into Sparrow Square's security camera system was illegal. Or immoral. Or irregular. Or something. What did she care?

He reached out to her keyboard and entered some code and, ah yes. There it was. A screen full of small tiles, each tile showing one section of Sparrow Square. The main entrance, the reception desk, the restaurants, corridors. "Which is our corridor?"

Bennett clicked on her keyboard until a corridor that looked exactly like all the other ones showed up, then was enlarged so that it filled the screen.

The corridor was empty. Well, yeah. Sparrow Square was made for businesspeople who wanted a home away from home. It was ten in the morning. The stay-in-beds would still be in bed, the workaholics were at work.

She stood and turned her laptop so he could see the screen. "Stay here, in front of my laptop. I'll be right back. I'll be in the corridor and you'll be able to see me the entire time. Or … not."

He glanced at her without moving his head, face turned to the monitor. "Okay."

Elle exited the apartment and walked slowly down the long corridor toward the elevator, touched it, and walked back. Like a lap, only not in a pool. Before she had a chance to knock at the door, it opened and there he was, Bennett, dark eyes lit up. Looking at her as if she were a magician. "I can't believe what I just saw!"

She smiled up at him. "Let me guess. My face was fuzzy, broken up with vertical lines or horizontal lines. Not clear at all and not recognizable as me."

"Bingo. I can't believe you did that. You're a genius."

She smiled smugly. "I know."

And he kissed her.

Five

Bennett's head did that sputtering thing her head had done on the monitor, like wires crossed. His head fizzled and flickered and sparked. Just like that, from his lips touching hers.

He was having a big big moment of cognitive dissonance, because kissing a principal was wrong on a million different levels and yet here he was, kissing Elle Castle like he was a man dying of thirst in the desert and he'd happened on an oasis.

It's not like he was kiss-starved or anything. Fuck no. He'd had sex … when was it? Not too long ago, with what's-her-name. The banker with the shark smile, who lectured him for an hour over dinner on interest rates.

But that was nothing like this. Fucking the banker was way less exciting than kissing Elle. She just sparkled with intelligence and life. That was when he was keeping his distance from her. And now kissing her … oh man.

Short circuit.

She was wriggling in his arms and like some distant scout frantically trying to signal that the enemy was on the horizon, his brain picked up on the fact that something was wrong. He loosened his hold — though it was the last thing he wanted to do — and she brought her arms up and wrapped them tightly around his neck.

Oh. She wanted to get closer, not get away.

These thoughts were vague and fleeting. What was front and center in his mind was how god-damned good she felt in his arms. How soft her lips were, her skin, how good she smelled. This was pleasure on some unknown scale, completely …

Their lips parted for a second while he angled his head for a better taste of her. But that second was just enough to break the electrical charge. He pulled his head back, closed his eyes. "We can't do this," he said, his voice rough. "It's … wrong."

He opened his eyes and saw her frown. *Wrong.* Wrong was the wrong word. The rusty cogs in his head creaked as they slowly turned. "Not wrong. Inappropriate."

She was still frowning so maybe inappropriate wasn't the right word either. He'd just exhausted the words file in his head so he kissed her again.

She kissed him back. Oh God, every time his tongue touched hers he felt a little electric shock. He walked her back one step, two, until her back hit the wall, and just dove in. His hands tunneled through that shiny black hair and cupped her head, holding her still for his kiss.

His mouth traveled from hers, down over the

sharp jawline to her long pale neck. He kissed her skin, licked it. God, she tasted absolutely delicious, like salty vanilla ice cream, so good he just had to take a bite. He gave her a tiny little nip, ending in a kiss right over the same spot and felt her give a little shudder.

Oh, yeah. She was sensitive there. And behind her ear. A nip there made her jump a little. A lick made her moan.

She was so responsive. He could feel what she was feeling. When he licked her neck he could feel the beat of her heart, fast and light. His hand smoothed over her shoulder, down over her left breast and he could feel her heartbeat there, harder and faster. He cupped her breast, rubbed his thumb over a hard nipple, and felt her excitement in her mouth as she exhaled on a moan.

Everything she did excited him while he went on an exploratory journey to see and feel what pleased her. She held all the power here, he was just along for the ride, because it all pleased him. Everything about her, the texture of her skin, the warmth of her mouth, it was all hot pleasure.

It took every ounce of self control he had to lift his mouth from her skin, though he wanted his mouth everywhere on her body. He wanted her naked and under him and because he wanted that really badly, he stopped, and breathed in her scent, trying to come back into himself.

Bennett held her close, one hand cupping her

head as it lay against his shoulder. Fuck yeah, it was inappropriate, but man, it felt good.

He didn't know how long they stood there. He could have stood there forever. But she finally gave a sigh and moved her head, looking up at him.

"Inappropriate?" she asked, arching one eyebrow.

Bennett shrugged. "Yeah. I'm supposed to protect you, not kiss you. As a matter of fact, I should fire myself."

"Are the two mutually exclusive? I mean, are you less likely to protect me now that we've kissed?"

"No. But it's unprofessional to get personally involved with a principal, with someone you're protecting. Throws your instincts off."

Her eyes searched his while she pondered this, frowning. Since she was thinking, he could look into her eyes without being creepy because man, they were the most beautiful eyes he'd ever seen. Such an unusual color …

"Do you wear contacts?" he blurted, the cogs in his head still in their rusty state, creaking restlessly.

"No." She frowned again. "You have a very erratic thought process."

No, he didn't. He was as linear as a ruler, normally. It was Elle Castle who threw him off his stride. But he couldn't say that. She couldn't help it if she was beautiful and fascinating.

With enormous difficulty, Bennett grabbed hold

of the remnants of self control he had left while releasing Elle. Releasing Elle was harder than he thought it would be and he found he had to actually step back, out of arm's length.

Elle put her fists on her hips. "Well?"

He stared at her. "Well, what?"

She frowned again and he realized she was doubting his intelligence. Or sanity. Or maybe both.

"Well, do we have an agreement or not?"

"What?" Bennett willed those rusty cogs into motion.

Elle gave a very unladylike snort. "We agreed that if I proved I could get to the pool for a swim anonymously, you'd let me go. You saw what my program did. No one would recognize me from that security tape."

Everything in his head fired back up, like the warp drive coming back online. He could think again. Though he had to wonder whether he'd gone temporarily insane, because he nodded. "Okay. You made your point. I'll accompany you down to the pool."

"Great. I'll be out right away." She gave him a smile so dazzling he almost stepped back again, and disappeared into the bedroom. Unlike most women she was really fast and came back out almost immediately.

He had to work to get his brain in alignment with his tongue.

Some instinct told him not to make any comments on how beautiful she looked but man … She had ordered a sleek dark blue racer's swimsuit, and was holding a cream cap in one hand. A thought was making its way slowly through his head, some kind of disconnect between her standing there in a one-piece bathing suit and walking down to the swimming pool wearing only that.

Before he could say anything, she snatched up a towel and terrycloth robe and shuffled into flip-flops. He looked down at the flip-flops and thought—*even her goddamn feet are beautiful.*

She was covered up. Thank God. Some primitive part of him was not happy at the thought of her walking through Sparrow Square in a bathing suit. She was just too … too … *too.*

Swim goggles dangled from a finger as she looked at him questioningly. "You're not going to swim?"

He had an answer for that. "Nope. I'm going to watch over you." He'd kissed her and that was already breaking protocol. Stripping down to swim briefs without a weapon, in the water, at a total disadvantage if anyone attacked them … not going to happen.

She thought that over. "Okay. I'm sorry, it would have been fun to have a swim together." She cocked her head as a thought occurred to her. "You *can* swim, though, right?"

Bennett had been a Navy SEAL for seven years

and would have continued if an ear injury hadn't made it impossible for him to go deep sea diving. He'd been drown-proofed — his instructors had thrown him into the deep end of a pool with hands and feet bound — and he'd survived. Every night they'd swum five miles in the dark freezing Pacific. He could swim underwater for fifty meters.

He deliberately didn't smile. "Yes, I can swim." He put a hand to her back. "Now let's go."

She didn't swim like a SEAL — that powerful sideways combat stroke that ate up the distance while churning the water as little as possible. No, she swam like a mermaid, gliding through the water with ease.

Bennett made himself comfortable on one of the expensive lounge chairs and watched her do her laps. It was his duty but it definitely wasn't a burden. They were alone in the pool, and he'd ensured that they'd stay alone by tying together the handles of the entrance with zip ties. Zip ties, together with C-4 and his Glock, were staples in his business. He didn't have any C-4 with him but he sure as hell had his Glock.

Being at the pool wasn't a hardship, either. It had been redesigned lately — his company had re-

ceived notification of an increase in condo costs —
and they'd gone back to a 1930s look. What the letter from the Sparrow Square administrators and
Elle called Art Deco. Intense colors, big terracotta
vases with thriving plants, scalloped edges everywhere. Comfortable chairs.

The entire huge room was visible at a glance.
And if anyone tried anything, he had the Glock in a
black shoulder holster that was invisible under his
black jacket, and a sharp knife in his boot. He'd
have to cut the plasticuffs holding the doors together without Elle noticing.

So. He could sit more or less assured that he
and his principal were safe and simply enjoy the
view. Elle gliding through the water, back and
forth, back and forth, as regular as a metronome.
In his head, he knew the usual number of laps a
normal, fit person would take and she was reaching
that point. He readied himself to get up and hand
her the big towel.

Actually, what he'd really like to do was wrap
her in the towel, rubbing those slim, sleek muscles
all over, then kiss her senseless. Actually, though,
he was the senseless one, because kissing a principal was such a huge no-no it was almost unthinka-
ble and yet all he could think about was doing it
again.

But she wasn't slowing down. She just kept on,
turning the water silver in her wake and as she continued her laps, way beyond the number for a nor-

mal workout, he realized what this was. He'd done it himself, numerous times. This morning in fact. She was easing her stress with exercise, the best stress release in the world.

Elle was being brave and remarkably cheerful about what was in essence a hole punched through her life, with no end in sight. God only knew how long it would take her asshole father to make up the money he'd lost. Being with Elle was anything but a hardship, but he was being paid while her entire life was on hold.

Halfway through the lap she veered toward him, clinging to the edge of the pool. She pushed her swim goggles up. She'd been swimming flat out for forty minutes and wasn't winded.

"Are we good? Do we need to get back?" She was trying to keep the anxiety out of her voice. Man, he understood. She felt free in the water.

Bennett crouched down and touched her hand. "Take as long as you want," he said gently. If anyone tried to come in while Elle was working through her stress, he'd just shoot them. "No problem."

She smiled, put her goggles back on, dipped below the surface and took off again. She swam for another half hour and was a tiny bit winded when she finally climbed the ladder out of the pool. Bennett was there, holding out the big towel. He wrapped it around her and because he wanted to wrap himself around her, he forced himself to step back.

"Thanks." She smiled up at him. "I really enjoyed that. And I really needed it. Thanks for letting me have my swim."

He understood completely. Bennett nodded. "You're welcome."

She cocked her head. "And now you feed me, correct?"

"Let's see if we can find something for lunch that won't harden your arteries. You've had a nice workout but it's pointless protecting you if you're going to drop dead of a heart attack."

She rolled her eyes as they reached the doors. "I'll eat a salad, mom. Promise."

Six

Elle disappeared into her room when they got back. Part of it was that she wanted to put the things she'd bought away neatly and start making this room her own. Part was staying away from Bennett.

She took a shower and then dressed in one of the pastel-colored yoga outfits she'd bought because it was clear they weren't going out. Sparrow Square had its own movie theater, apparently — two actually. One for first-run movies and the other for classic movies. Bennett would probably nix going to the movies, even if inside the complex. But the in-house entertainment system was vast and if she got bored she could order a movie for the huge flat-screen TV on the wall. There was a menu of movies and TV shows on the dresser and it was impressive. There were films in every language known to man and in every genre there was. But she didn't want to watch a movie.

She wasn't bored but she was restless, even after an unusually long swim. Normally, swimming calmed her down if she was stressed or frustrated. She was both stressed *and* frustrated. Stressed because she was essentially in lockdown for an unspecified period of time and frustrated because she was in lockdown with the sexiest man she'd ever been near, who clearly thought that fraternizing with his protectee — no, his *principal* — was forbidden.

The thing was — he was right.

Them having an affair under these circumstances was inappropriate — his word — and stupid — her word. Though Bennett had set them up in iron-tight secure circumstances, shit happened. Shit happened all the time and they should stay vigilant.

Ordinarily, she never had frustrated desire. She didn't desire many men and those few she'd wanted had luckily wanted her right back. Elle never let sexual desire waylay her. It wasn't a big element of her life, which is why what she felt for Bennett was like a punch in the stomach. And totally out of character.

Apart from the sheer animal attraction — which was huge — the alarming thing was that she liked the man. He was appealing and smart. All those muscles and brains. It was heady. Elle was used to male intelligence linked to scrawniness and awkwardness.

He just … blindsided her. He didn't often smile but when he did — watch out. An actual dimple carved itself into one of his lean cheeks and she went weak-kneed. It was alarming, as if someone else had been lying dormant inside her body, waiting for the right guy to take over the controls.

Like, right now. She emerged from her room just as he was setting the table. Tall and handsome and domesticated. And right under that domesticated surface was a warrior.

Just look at him, she thought, as he finished setting the table, focused and efficient. She was sure he was just as focused and efficient when on the shooting range and in bed.

Whoa. Where had that thought come from?

He looked up from the table at her and it felt like she'd been punched hard. That dark gaze was powerful and penetrating, eyes slightly narrowed. It was as if he were walking around inside her head — and she sincerely hoped he couldn't because she was thinking embarrassing thoughts.

Those last few steps to the table were like walking through molasses, time stretching out as he watched her. Elle slid into her seat, grateful that she made it in time to salvage her dignity. Her knees were about ready to give out.

Her hands trembled as she billowed out the huge heavy linen napkin and placed it on her lap.

Bennett lifted one silver dome to uncover a soup tureen. "I took the liberty of ordering, I hope that's ok. If there's anything you don't like, we can order something else."

His brow was furrowed and he spoke gravely, as if the thought of her not liking what he ordered was actually painful.

She smiled. "I like good food, but I'm not fussy. Whatever it is, it smells good. What did you order?"

He ladeled some soup into her bowl. "Spelt soup

with a small salad. And I ordered BLTs for both of us, since you eat meat."

"Bacon isn't meat," she said, picking up her spoon. "It's a necessity."

He made the most extraordinary sound. A little bit like a suppressed laugh, a little like a lion's purr, and it was like a hand caressing her. Oh, man. She put a spoonful of the soup in her mouth before she used her mouth to say something embarrassing like — make that sound again. Or — touch me. Please.

And then she made her own sound. Startled pleasure. "This is really good."

He started eating, too. "It is. We can cook for ourselves, too, once we've exhausted the menu. I'm not a bad cook. Do you cook?"

Elle smiled at the thought. "Not at all," she said cheerfully. "I can make soft boiled eggs if I have a timer. Make coffee and tea and toast. Peel fruit. That's about it. Sorry."

He shrugged, one side of his mouth lifting. "No problem. I placed a big order for food supplies, so we won't be dependent on the restaurants here. We'll have plenty of time. At the end I'll be making ossobuco that stews for ten hours and we'll be playing endless games of Monopoly. And before you say anything —" his big hand shot up, palm facing her. "No, I don't know how long we'll be here. That is completely out of my control, as I said."

That was exactly what she was going to ask.

"Never even thought of asking it," she said.

The truth was, it wasn't so bad being cooped up with Bennett Cameron in a deluxe apartment with every comfort known to man. He was such good company, easy to get on with and immensely attractive.

But beyond that — he was good at his job because she felt *protected*. It had never occurred to her that that was a thing. Elle wasn't fearful by nature, but she was a woman who lived alone and moved in a man's world. She traveled often, sometimes to difficult places, and she traveled alone.

It wasn't always fun and it wasn't always safe. Unease was like a background noise. She realized that because right now she felt *safe*. Even if there were a zombie apocalypse, he'd keep her safe and get her out of London and find them a nice little house in the country ...

This was crazy thinking, but the feeling of safety persisted and it was warm and soft and incredibly nice.

"So," she said, taking her first bite of the sandwich and finding it delicious. "Bodyguarding, huh?"

He smiled. "Like I said, in the business we call it 'close protection', but it's essentially bodyguarding, yeah."

He looked so amazingly super competent, like he could fend off those zombie hordes while cooking ossobuco, sipping a martini. And then there was that ramrod straight posture, that no nonsense demeanor.

"Did you train for that in the military?"

His dark eyes were amused as he nodded his head. "Bingo. Among other things."

"What ..." What were they called? Not departments, that was university. Not Sections or Offices. Branches, that was it. "What branch?"

"Navy. I was in the Navy until I had to quit because of an injury." A shadow crossed his face, almost too fleeting to see. Elle was surprised that she'd seen it, she wasn't always tuned in to the emotions of her fellow humans. Whatever the injury was, it wasn't visible. He looked superbly fit.

"Navy, huh." She looked up suddenly. "What part of the navy?"

"I was a SEAL," he said and frowned when she dropped her head into her hands and gave a low moan. "What's wrong?"

"Oh, my God. I asked if you could *swim*. I asked a navy SEAL if he could *swim*. And — I was even showing off a little for you. I am such a dope." Her face was on fire.

When she let her hands fall to the table, he covered one of them with his again. His hand was so beautiful. Huge, callused, warm. Strong. "Well, you couldn't know. And to tell you the truth, I was impressed."

Yeah, right. She gave an unladylike snort. Strong fingers gently caught her chin and lifted her face to his. If she'd expected a sneer, it wasn't there.

"I admired your — your swim form."

She blinked.

He tilted his head and gave a half smile. "And because I'm not dead, I also admired your *form* form, if you get what I mean."

Elle watched his eyes, dark and warm and full of humor. Yeah, she got what he meant. It was funny. She usually disliked compliments on her looks. She'd been lucky enough to take after her mother who was still a beauty at fifty-five. She thanked the goddesses every day that she didn't take after her father, who looked like a cross between a goat and Gollum. Her looks didn't have anything to do with *her*, with her abilities and strengths. So she usually brushed compliments off, particularly since they were often given by men she cared nothing about.

She couldn't say that about Bennett. He intrigued her and, well, she admired his ... form, too. Broad shoulders, thick pecs visible beneath the sweater, lean waist, long strong legs, what was not to like? And she felt at ease with him, as if they'd known each other for a long time instead of 36 hours, even if some of that time had included him drugging her and lashing her to a chair.

Not exactly a great first date.

She wanted to know more and it looked like he wasn't going anywhere. "So." Elle rested her chin in her hand. "How does one transition from being a navy SEAL to a bodyguard? Or close protector, or whatever you call yourself."

"Close protection agent. And it's a natural transition. We did a lot of that in the Teams. We provided protection for a lot of bigwigs coming in from Washington. They needed a protection detail which we provided. And we also went in to save people under threat and bring them out. You got points if you did that and the hostage stayed alive. When I got out, I founded a company to do what I had already done for Uncle Sam. Only the pay was better."

"How many … agents work for you?"

"About a hundred fifty. We're going to get a new intake of about fifty more operators very soon, business is booming. It's a messed-up world. Good for business."

She chewed that over in her mind. "Were you happy with the transition from the military to civilian life?"

Again, that something, a kind of shadow, passed over his features, but when he answered it was still in that light-hearted tone. "It's okay. We — my operators and I — worked in a world where war is a constant. We've been at war for over seventeen years, much longer than I've been in the service. And we're still at war and we're not winning. What we do now, in the company — well, we win. We keep people alive, which is the mission." Another light shadow, like a fleeting cloud across the sun. "Until —"

"Until?"

Bennett sighed, pushed the cup of coffee to one side and clasped his hands in front of him. He looked down at them for a long time, so long she wondered what was going through his head. Whether he was going to continue or not.

He lifted his head. "There are things on the horizon that are worrying us." He closed his eyes, opened them again, fierce and dark. "That's a dumb word. There are things on the horizon that scare us all shitless."

Bennett Cameron didn't look like a man scared of much on this earth. If it scared *him* … "Like?"

"We haven't lost a principal yet, though some day we will. It's just the odds. You can't really protect a principal against a sniper who is accurate at a mile out. He is invisible and the bullet arrives before the sound of the shot reaches you. And there is research into programmable bullets. Bullets that can be shot from miles away and can change trajectory to hit the target, just like a miniature heat-seeking missile. Weaponized drones are a nightmare. Or drones carrying DNA sniffers. Likewise, there isn't an armored car built that can withstand a strike by an RPG. That's a —"

"Rocket propelled grenade." She nearly smiled at his surprised expression. He had no idea how many hours she spent playing Call of Duty 4. "Go on."

"Basically we keep principals alive through stealth. Through making sure no one knows where they are. But sometimes we have principals that are too stupid to live. Like the daughter of a rich Colombian who'd survived two kidnapping attempts. We took the job on and took her to a safe house and believe me when I say the safe house was *safe*. But the girl had a boyfriend she was hot for and she smuggled in a cellphone and called him. Turns out he was the one who'd ordered the kidnappings. Luckily one of my officers heard her talking and got everyone out of there about an hour before the whole place blew up. How do you protect yourself against human stupidity?"

"You can't," she said crisply. "All you can do is work the odds and leave as little room for stupidity as possible."

He nodded.

"So, what are the plans?"

He'd been staring at the tabletop, clearly depressing himself. He looked at her without raising his head. "I beg your pardon?"

"Seems to me that your business is coming up against a technological wall. Major disruption. It wouldn't be the first business and it won't be the last. But you also seem like the kind of guy who doesn't sit still for a tsunami of tech to overwhelm him. So what's Plan B?"

Bennett gave a half smile. "What makes you think there's a Plan B?"

She just sat silently, looking at him. Why he'd have a Plan B (and C and D, probably) was self-evident in the way he held himself. In his sharp, observant gaze and the way he moved, with 360° awareness. After a minute or two, he sighed.

"You're right. There is a Plan B. I'm looking into expanding into other areas. Areas where human intelligence matters. Tech supported of course, but where the odds are more in our favor."

"Okay," she said. "Like?"

"Well, we're specialized abroad. It's why head-quarters is in London, because it's a really good time zone for global operations. So we're becoming the go-to company for things like international surveil-lance, tracking down cross-border fugitives, infiltrat-ing companies under investigation."

"And you're good at it." It wasn't a question.

"We do okay." He leaned forward a little. "As a matter of fact, your software would be amazingly use-ful to us. I'd love to be able to move my operators in areas where there are video cams without being ID'd. Would you be willing to sell it to me?"

"No." Her voice was decisive.

He didn't even blink. A businessman used to ne-gotiating. "I could make it really worth your while."

She shook her head. Nuh-uh.

"Really *really* worth your while." He wasn't whee-dling, but close to it.

"If it's money you're offering, I don't need mon-ey."

It was true. A mountain of untouched money had been deposited by her father in her name at Chase Manhattan. She didn't touch it. But it was there, even though she didn't need it. She guest-taught under contract at various universities and they paid really well. Her two books were academic bestsellers and her conference speaker fees were high. No, she didn't need money.

"But …" She leaned forward a little, too. Exactly as much as he had, no more no less. Two could play the negotiating game. As a matter of fact, Elle was probably better at it. "I'd be willing to barter for it."

That did surprise him, though he didn't show it. Not a muscle moved. But his eyes blinked without blinking.

"Okay." He didn't move his gaze from her eyes as he opened his big hands on the table, as if ready to receive something. "Shoot."

"I'll happily give you the use of my program and I'll throw in, say, five training days for your best IT guy. Who I don't think is you."

He didn't wince, didn't change expression, but his eyes lit up with what looked like amusement. "No, not me. So, just to be clear, you're willing to give me a program that can mask my operatives when entering places with security cams, which will make a huge difference to them, maybe even save lives. Plus training my best IT tech, which would be Melissa Sanders. And in return you don't want money?"

She nodded. "That about sums it up."

"I hardly dare ask what it is you do want in return. Is it illegal? Immoral?"

"Not even fattening. I want you to assign me a problem you're dealing with that isn't close protection. I wouldn't be trained in that in any way and it feels … boring."

He tilted his head, looking intrigued. "Boring isn't

the word most people would use for close protection."

"But it is. Every aspect of it is out of your control except your own vigilance. You guys must drown in cortisol while on the job. And I should imagine most principals are people with more money than sense and certainly not interesting people. So you lay your lives on the line daily for, essentially, jerks. I'm sure it is very well paid and you'll have plenty of work. People with money tend to have lots of enemies. But somehow I don't see you as driven by money lust. So you're tired of doing something just because it pays well and you'd like to do something other than protecting jerks. Is that an accurate description?"

"It is." He sighed. "But don't say I said that. And present company excepted, of course."

"Of course." She tilted her head to study him, exactly as he had. "You don't seem like the kind of guy to stay with an unsatisfactory situation for long. So tell me more about your Plan B."

It was a full blown smile now. "You don't pull your punches, do you?"

"That's a stupid expression — to pull your punches. It comes from boxing. And either you're fighting, so you'd be dumb to pull your punches, or you're not fighting and you'd be a sociopath if you were punching someone."

He threw back his head and laughed. She'd have been offended except for the fact that he was amazingly hot when he laughed. His eyes — which she saw now were dark gray and not dark brown — crinkled and he flashed amazingly white teeth. How could he have been a soldier with those amazing teeth? Had he never been punched? She'd lost a tooth when she was twelve because she'd tripped over a tree trunk, and playing in the yard was much safer than being a navy SEAL.

Bennett reached out a long finger and traced a line between her eyebrows. "Those look like complicated thoughts. I assure you I'm an uncomplicated man."

Oh no, he wasn't. He had complication written all over that handsome face.

God, she could almost feel the lines of attraction, and at the end of those lines were tiny virtual grasping hands pulling her forward toward him. She had to actually clutch the edges of the table to keep from getting up and sitting down on his lap.

This was so unlike her.

Though, to be fair, he was immensely attractive. Elle met a lot of single men in her line of work, but she didn't meet too many attractive men. And absolutely nobody like Bennett Cameron.

Still, she didn't want him laughing at her, either. "So tell me what the new Plan B is."

He stopped laughing and looked down at the tabletop, head hanging between broad shoulders. He looked like he was chewing on a problem. She waited while he chewed his way to a solution.

"Okay," he said finally, head coming back up. The

laughter had been completely wiped off his face. "I've built up a company that happens to have a lot of latent expertise in things other than close protection. Like I said, we operate throughout the world and a lot of my operators are familiar with foreign countries. We've got deep knowledge of Africa, Asia and Europe. Two of my guys who grew up in Alaska and were originally part of the Army's 10th Mountain Division pulled off a difficult mission in Antarctica. So we're ... expanding our portfolio, as it were. Mainly investigative work for the government or private clients."

Spying, she imagined he meant. A shiver of excitement went through her.

This was it. "Okay. There you go. That's my price."

He cocked his head again, a gesture she was beginning to recognize, tilting his head to perceive better. "What?"

"I told you. You want my program? Give me a case. Give me a case to study or to solve, something that can be done via computer and not in the field, of course." She waved at the four taupe walls. "I'm a little hampered at the moment. Plus I'm not what you'd call a 'field person'. I do my best work in dark dens, with order-in pizza. But I'll bet you have something in the pipeline I could work on."

Bennett was staring at her, humor gone, scowling.

A bell rang in the kitchen. She could almost see him refraining from saying *saved by the bell*. Though he clearly thought it. His face cleared up and he pushed himself to his feet.

"That's the carrot muffins. And as far as giving you one of our cases—absolutely not."

Elle rose, smiling. Those muffins smelled delicious. She'd have those wonderful carrot muffins and then bug Bennett until he gave her what she wanted. Mentally rubbing her hands, she thought — *this is going to be fun.*

Seven

She broke him. Bennett thought of himself as essentially unbreakable. His Senior Chief hadn't managed to break him during Hell Week, though he'd tried real hard. Senior Chief Darryl 'Rattlesnake' Murray had made it his personal goal to make Bennett ring the bell, the signal that the candidate quit, but he never managed it.

Bennett had faced any number of enemies whose one goal in life was to see him dead and buried, and he'd come out the victor.

Dr. Elle Castle just defeated him.

She ate his muffins with gusto, chattering away, fixing him with those enormous cobalt eyes, blinding him with science and flooding him with well-thought-out arguments in her soft, expressive voice.

It was like being bludgeoned to death by butterfly wings.

Finally Bennett put down his fork, rolled his eyes to the ceiling — which provided no help whatsoever — and caved.

She was on a roll. "Theory is a remarkably useful underpinning for objective action —"

"Okay," he said, restraining himself from throwing up his hands.

"— and provides a useful analytical tool to — what did you say?" She froze, a forkful of her third muffin halfway to her mouth. Bennett had no idea how she wasn't 400 pounds with all the food she ate. But she wasn't. She was slender with a few perfect curves in all the right places.

He sighed. "I said okay. I imagine you are prepared to hound me day and night until I give in, anyway."

"Absolutely." She patted her mouth with the monogrammed linen napkin, probably hiding a smile. "I like getting my way."

"I bet." Bennett said sourly.

It was an act. The truth was, he was looking forward to working with her. Looking forward to watching all that formidable brainpower brought to bear on a problem that was vexing him and his company. Maybe she could help. God knows, after gnawing on it for a month they weren't any closer to a resolution. "Let me finish clearing off the table and I can give you the details of an issue we have."

He had to avert his eyes because she simply glowed. No other word for it. It looked like a spotlight had lit up behind her eyes.

She stood. "Absolutely not. You can clear the table any time. First, give me the parameters of the mission."

The parameters of the mission. He sighed again

but went obediently into his room to get his own laptop, secretly smiling. This was going to be good.

He set his laptop up on the desk next to hers. He looked at the two computers, then looked at her. "Next to your laptop, mine looks like a caveman's club."

She smiled at him, pleased, and all he could do was stare and clench his fists. Goddamn, she was irresistible. You'd have to be dead to resist her, and Bennett wasn't dead, he was very much alive. He could feel the blood pulsing in his veins and heat coursing through his body at her nearness. This close her skin looked like velvet, a magnet for his hands. He curled them and mentally handcuffed himself.

The memory of their kiss was still vivid. The taste of her and the feel of her were imprinted on his brain, a really primitive part of it.

No touching the principal. It would have been rule number one if he'd ever been tempted. As it was, he'd always thought that rule number one was *No punching the principal* because, God, he'd been tempted. Some principals were fucking impossible.

Elle sure wasn't. Right now, in fact, she was quivering with eagerness to help him.

Bennett glanced over at her open laptop and stared. She'd put in a password and instead of defaulting to Google like every other laptop he'd ever seen, the screen was dark with just a small white search field in the center. She saw his look and smiled. "The dark web."

Bennett didn't say anything. He was supposed to be an expert but he rarely used the dark web. Frankly didn't know how to use it well.

Everything about her computer was special, unique. No logos. Matte, dark gray surface that looked non-reflective and dense, like an alien space-ship.

"Yours is better than mine," he said.

"Yes." She looked at him and smirked. "It's like the Maserati of computers."

"Fast?"

"Like lightning. Almost quantum in its computing power."

He sighed, torn between lust for her and for her computer. "I suppose you wouldn't sell it to me?"

Her face morphed instantly, turning serious and somber. Her entire body tensed. "I … can't. This computer was smuggled out of Shanghai and there are only three of them in the world."

Wow. Okay. "Really?"

"Gotcha." Elle laughed and relaxed. "No. I was just yanking your chain. It's a beta product of a small company founded by three kids who studied under me, so I get to test-run the prototype. I think the company's going to be big. I think it will be the equivalent of Apple in 2030. Maybe sooner."

Bennett sighed and felt ancient, a relic of another age. Some kids who had *been her students* had created a computer that made him feel like a Neanderthal in a cave.

He was pushing forty and she made him feel like he was pushing eighty.

Still … judging by the woodie pulsing under the table, not all of him felt eighty. His hard-on felt fourteen and uncontrollable.

She turned smiling to him, deep blue eyes glowing, fingers laid gently along the sides of her computer, a little like a gunman keeping his trigger finger alongside the trigger, not inside the trigger guard. Waiting.

Bennett wasn't a fool. This was a challenge. That was okay. He was used to challenges. Hell, his entire military career had been one long challenge after another. And building his globe-spanning security business into the billion-dollar behemoth it was today had been another huge challenge.

Good thing he liked challenges.

"Hit me," Elle said, smiling and … oh God. He closed his eyes because the image those words conjured up was entirely sexual. She was dressed in one of those clingy light-colored yoga outfits and they outlined her shape lovingly. Caressed those perfect breasts, dipped in at her tiny waist, swelled at her hips, outlined her long, slender legs.

Sex. It was right there, on the table. Maybe even their laptops were infused with it. He sure was infused with it. Very vivid images, with sensorial input, of Elle spread out on her bed with the royal blue bedspread that matched her eyes filled his head. She was naked, all that smooth creamy skin a magnet for his hands and his mouth. She held up her arms for him and he covered her, entering her …

"Bennett?" She frowned.

Dear sweet God. What was wrong with him? He pulled every ounce of self control he had out of his ass and turned to her. "Sorry. Got a little distracted … by your laptop. So you want a real world problem to solve?"

She nodded, sleek black hair swinging against her neck. "Tell me everything."

"Okay." So. He was really going to do this. "We have a guy who has gone missing."

Elle nodded. "Okay. A good guy or a bad guy?"

The thought of Arthur Kudlow wiped the smile from his face. "Bad guy. Greedy guy. The worst."

Her face turned serious. "Okay."

He was telling it wrong. Start from the *beginning*, he thought. "This guy, we'll call him Mr. X, has disappeared with a whole bunch of files that are doing a lot of harm. The files contain sensitive economic and security data, which is what he stole them for, but they also contain the names of people cooperating with the US in countries around the world. Some nasty countries where we need friends. This is what happened to one of them. Last week."

Bennett typed in a command that brought up a photograph. It was one of the more presentable ones of the damage Kudlow had done. It showed a man lying face down on a dusty street, face turned slightly to the right. A big puddle of something dark and oily spread under him. It didn't take much to realize that the puddle was blood and that the man was dead.

Bennett didn't want to show her the other photos. Some had missing limbs. One a missing head. One man had been strangled with his own entrails. No, this was the only one he would show her.

"This is one of the men who has died as a result of these files?" Elle turned to him, eyes wide.

"One of them." Bennett's jaws clenched.

"Mr. X got the files from his job?"

He nodded.

"Where did he work?"

"At a three-letter agency."

She cocked her head. "They are all three letter agencies, Bennett. CIA, NSA, DHS, DEA ..."

He held up a hand. Pointless being coy with Elle Castle. "NSA."

"So, he was an analyst."

"Yeah. And a good one."

"I understand analysts."

It hit him that she *would* understand analysts. More than he would. They operated on a different wavelength. "You probably do. More than I do."

"Probably." She said it without any vanity whatsoever. A fact of life. "Bennett. Let's cut to the chase. I imagine your Mr. X has disappeared and that you have been tasked with finding him. I also imagine you have checked, using facial recognition, all the airports and bus stations and train stations. Though if he is willing to sell his country out for money, he's not taking a Greyhound bus to a small town in North Dakota where he will disappear to a shack in the woods. He's abroad somewhere."

Bennett nodded. "Our conclusions exactly."

"So. He flew out of the country. When did he disappear?"

"A month ago."

"You've checked all private airfields, right? He might have chartered a jet. Hell, if he is being paid enough, he might have bought himself a jet."

Damn. It had taken him and his operatives 24 hours to think of that one, a private jet. But at least they had. He wasn't going to be too humiliated. "Yeah. We caught him. Flying out of a private airfield in Connecticut, on a chartered jet. He had a valid passport, in a fake name. He filed a flight plan but the data was lost. Wiped out from the servers. And the pilot has disappeared. We lost him after that."

"He'll have another name and another passport and probably another identity. If he deals with data, he'll know how to do that."

Bennett nodded glumly. "We are scouring the world. There is some pressure on us to find him. Not just from the agency. We're anxious too. There are lives at stake. Brave men and women are going to be betrayed."

"You're going to have to give me all your files on this man, plus his real name."

He said nothing.

"Bennett." Her voice was gentle. "Data is a fingerprint. It's identity. And anyway, his life and his name from before are gone. But I'd like to analyze who he was."

He still didn't say anything.

"If it helps, I have a TS/SCI security clearance."

That jolted him out of his paralysis. "You what?" It was the level of security clearance he'd had as a SEAL. "I thought you were a games theorist."

"I've been called in several times by — a three letter agency," she said primly, looking at him out of the corner of her eye. "They needed help with some algorithms. You can give me data without transgressing the terms of your contract with your own agency. Technically, I could be an outside contractor. Happens all the time."

He let out a breath. Giving her the name of the shithead would have violated his contract. He would have given in eventually because he wanted Kudlow stopped in the worst way, but it would have eaten at his conscience. A little. But now …

"I'll email you all the files we have on him. Arthur Kudlow. I imagine you can receive them securely?"

She smiled. "If your laptop were as good as my laptop, you could have transferred those files by tapping your computer to mine." She shifted her space-age laptop a little so the corner touched his laptop. That kind of feature was years away for mere civilians like him. "But it's not. Give me your email and I'll send you a path to follow to send me everything you have on this guy, this Arthur Kudlow. The pathway is absolutely secure."

She did and he did and then she did the damndest thing.

She disappeared.

One minute she was there and the next she wasn't.

Her body was there, slender and still as a statue, but her spirit had disappeared inside her magic computer.

She sat, for hours, moving only to key in commands from the keyboard and use the mouse, eyes tracking what was on her screen.

Bennett was able to follow at first, because she was perusing the files on Arthur Kudlow that he'd sent her. Then she accessed an app of her own and he lost her. The screen was filled mainly with numbers and formulae and algorithms. She was absorbing information faster than the speed of light. There wasn't much he could do from this point on as his beautiful witch worked her magic.

He got up, cleared the table, loaded the dishwasher, and prepped dinner. He could have ordered in but, somehow he didn't want to. There was a magical atmosphere in the apartment, as if they were closed up in their own bower, and he didn't want any intrusions, not even a waiter delivering meals to them.

While dinner was cooking — minestrone to be paired with baked cheese — he changed into his gym clothes and had another satisfying hour in the apartment's gym. Worked some sexual tension out of his system, too. Then showered.

When he put a cup of tea beside her, she took three sips, absent-mindedly, then pushed the cup away to write something on a piece of paper. An hour later, he put a fresh cup of tea next to her hand and over the next hour she finished it.

There was complete silence but it wasn't cold. He knew all about cold silences, which is what reigned in his own apartment after coming back from a long mission. Dead, chill silence. No, this silence was calm. He was surprised he couldn't hear the clacking of her brain, because it felt like he should. He could almost see vibrations around it.

Bennett had once dated a beautiful but flaky woman who had shifted all his furniture around because she said his apartment had terrible feng-shui, and then filled it with crystals, promising him they would absorb bad vibes and replace them with good ones.

The only thing that came of that relationship was bruised shins because he kept bumping into his furniture in the dark. There was no noticeable change in the vibes of his home.

But here ... yeah. It had felt good when he came out of the gym to see Elle quietly absorbed, working with utter focus, like some genius fairy come down to earth to help him find that fucker Kudlow. She almost shimmered, and gave off very good vibes.

After his shower, he'd sat down at his own computer and got through a lot of pending business and cleared his slate at around five in the afternoon. He felt good and relaxed, all caught up. So he was sitting in one of the apartment's very comfortable armchairs, reading a history of modern China he'd been meaning to get to, when he looked up in surprise.

Elle had made a sound of triumph and was sitting back, smiling, picking up the croissant left over from breakfast he'd put beside her and which she'd ignored up until now. "Got him!" she exclaimed.

Bennett was usually fast on the uptake but he'd been immersed in China's Cultural Revolution with Mao killing off a big segment of his people, and had to take a moment to focus. Thank God he didn't say *got who?* Because that would have been embarrassing.

"I have Arthur Kudlow," Elle said and beckoned to him with a finger. "Come see."

He put down his iPad and walked over to her. He stood behind her, one hand on her delicate shoulder. He bent so his face was next to hers and looked at her laptop screen and *ohmygod, there he was!*

Arthur Kudlow.

Fatter, sunburned and happy, with his hand on the red fender of a car. It was impossible to make out the make of car and where he was.

Elle clicked and the date of the picture and its GPS coordinates appeared. The date was three days ago and the coordinates — he started calculating in his head.

"Bali," Elle said. "He's in Bali."

Bennett tightened his hold on her shoulder. Not enough to hurt but enough to say — you're staying with me. I'm not letting you go. She'd solved a problem in something like six hours that he and his crew hadn't been able to solve in a month. And she hadn't broken a sweat.

"You're a miracle worker," he said, bending down to look her in the face. She smiled, pleased. A tiny little blush pinked her cheeks and oh God, he was a goner. "Walk me through it."

Elle pointed at the extra chair and he scooted it over to her until he too was in front of Puff the Magic Computer and he was sitting so close to her their legs touched. Lines of electricity ran up and down his thigh.

She brought up a screen which was incomprehensible. Then, as it came into focus, he could see it was a sort of cloud. He could make out chunks of data and how they connected with each other. Her monitor was amazingly sharp, the images carefully delineated, the colors bright.

Looking closer, he could see that she had made a cloud of Kudlow's life.

"I suspect that you and your team were looking for him from his moment of disappearance on, am I right? Trying to project your way forward to where he'd gone to ground?"

"Yeah. We've been scanning airports and train stations throughout the world but man, it's a lot of data."

"An almost impossible amount of data and you'd need a lot of time and massive number crunching power to do it. But it's a huge blunt instrument, when you can use a scalpel."

Bennett shook his head in admiration. Go, Elle. "Show me."

"Okay, I turned the problem on its head and started with the man himself. What he wants, what motivates him."

"Hell," Bennett said in disgust. "I can tell you that. Money. He's a greedy fuck." He gave her a sideways glance. "Sorry."

"Well, yes, from what I could see he *is* a greedy fuck. So I put all the elements of his life in a cloud format and yes, he does seem to be highly motivated by money. He was constantly in debt and constantly buying new things, things he really didn't need. He was a member of a golf club where membership cost $80,000 a year and he went exactly four times. He's flipped three houses in the past five years, only he managed to buy high and sell low. But digging deeper, besides crass materialism, he is fascinated by Ferraris."

Bennett blinked.

"Huh." That wasn't in Kudlow's profile at all. How did they miss it? "He owned a Ferrari?" They definitely should have caught that.

"He wished. No. But he had a fanboy level of fanaticism. He belonged to a number of online forums where there was passionate discussion — to the point of death threats — on the thickness of lacquer finishes and what was the best model Ferrari in 1956 and whether the ironblock is better than the F140."

"God," he said.

She looked over at him primly, mouth fighting a smile. "I wonder whether you might belong to gun forums where they fight over technical specifications."

Bennett sighed. "Busted."

To her credit, there was no snark. She just kept tapping away, pulling up page after page, which went up as tiles on the screen. She pointed at the tiles as she spoke. "Okay, so I broke down the data. Here you have the number of hours he was online after work. An average of five hours. Some days more, some days less, but that's the mean. Here you have what he spent his time on and you can see that he spent 94% of his time on Ferrari forums, another 4% on the Ferrari site and 2% on porn sites. Those are not average figures. Most men spend at least 8% of their online time on porn sites."

She cast him a sideways glance.

Bennett held his hands up. "Don't look at me. I spend 0 hours scouting out porn." It was true. He gave up porn at fifteen when he discovered that real life women were way more fun and much prettier than what could be seen in magazines or online.

She gave a faint smile. "So. Our guy frequented no news sites at all. Presumably he got all the news he needed at work. Then I broke down his presence on the forums. He used a program to cloak his IP, but for an NSA guy he was fairly easy to follow. He didn't put real work into hiding his IP. He just used avatars, like most of the other guys on the forums. Discussions are weird. It sometimes gets a little freaky when it's not super nerdy. His deep desire to own a Ferrari is palpable on all the forums. And look here."

She pointed to one of the tiles in the center of the screen. It was a photograph of a pudgy male hand, palm open, indicating a shelf of … something. Some objects. Bennett leaned closer.

"I took a high-density photo of the thumb and index figure, turned them into 3D images and compared them to the prints on file of Arthur Kudlow. They match. And check out those shelves." With a click of her mouse that looked like it was made out of titanium, the tile zoomed out and Bennett could see three rows of shiny, red … things.

Another click and the tile zoomed out even more and now he could see that the shiny red things were replica cars. Ferraris. At least forty of them, remarkably well made.

"Most of those are collectors' items and cost at least $1,000 each, sometimes more," Elle said. "I checked."

"Jesus." Bennett did a quick calculation in his head. "Huh. So on those three rows must be —"

"Almost fifty thousand dollars' worth of replica models."

"Fifty thousand dollars' worth of *toys?*" Bennett asked, aghast.

"The collectors definitely don't consider them toys. They are stand-ins for the real thing and there were four days of forum debate on the color of the sidewalls. It's a whole world and it's not too healthy."

"Apparently not." He gave a side glance to Elle. "Kudlow disappeared but didn't take his expensive toys with him."

"No, he didn't. And I think I know why. Anyway, the next tile —" Her mouse moved and the tile instantly blew up. "The next tile is a publication. Our Kudlow is a subscriber to ENZO, which is a magazine dedicated to the original designer, Enzo Ferrari. The subscription to the paper magazine is in his name. He canceled it eight weeks ago. He also canceled tickets to a Formula 1 race in Texas. He didn't get his money back."

"He was already planning his escape," Bennett said.

Elle nodded. "I think he realized that he might have something that would make all his money problems go away forever and that might be better than a subscription to a magazine."

Bennett looked at her. "The files."

"Mmm. According to your data he disappeared a month ago. So his last known location is on an outbound chartered private jet bound for Paris. And then the flight plan disappeared."

"That's right." It burned. It burned that they

hadn't been able to trace him, knowing the destination, though they'd brought major crunching power to the chase. One of his operatives had even gone to Paris Orly with several photographs but Kudlow's passport wasn't in the system as having landed and facial recognition run through the security cameras came up empty. Everyone in the company was frustrated.

"I know he disappeared between Connecticut and Paris, somehow. And I think you and your company have probably run through every possible permutation, have thought of every contingency, trying to figure out where he's gone and how he got there."

"Yup," he confirmed gloomily. "Put in thousands of hours. Like I said, the pilot has disappeared, as well. Either he was paid to disappear or Kudlow disappeared him. They didn't land in Paris."

"Well, I didn't try to replicate what you guys are doing, that would be duplication of effort. What I did was make the leap forward. He has to be somewhere. Setting aside the problem of how he got there, where is he *now?* That's what we really need to know."

Those glowing eyes caught his and for a second wiped out the thinking part of his brain until he shook himself back into the moment. Damn. *Concentrate.* "Okay."

"So —" she blew up another tile. "Presuming that Kudlow changed his coordinates but not his personality, I pulled on the Ferrari thread. Because one thing is clear. He now has the money to indulge his passion. From what you say, he has plenty of it."

"Yeah." Bennett's jaws clenched. "And that money is blood money."

She shot him a quick glance of understanding. "That's why it's important to get him. And ... I have."

He leaned forward instantly. "That photo of him. Show me again."

"First, let me describe the steps I took to get there. It's important."

She wasn't showing off, that was clear. And Bennett did want to hear how she got there. Another few minutes wasn't going to change anything. He was definitely going to learn something here. "Okay. Show me."

"Right. I started from here." Another tile, this with various words of different sizes. A word cloud. The larger the word the more often that word appeared. The largest word was Ferrari. The words that were the next size down were all related to the cars or manufacturer. Other words were tiny. "He has an interest in 1980s pop, God knows why. He did some research for the purchase of a designer jacket, settled on Ralph Lauren. And has an interest in the actress Anne Hathaway. But overwhelmingly, he is interested in Ferraris, in every aspect of them. In fact —" she pulled up another tile, "here is the breakdown of time spent. Like I said before, he spends on average five hours a day on the internet, 4.7 hours on Ferrari-related topics. I traced three avatars on the forums, particularly obsessed, back to him. Their handles are Piero, Dino and Alfredo. Enzo Ferrari's son, father and brother. Kudlow doesn't seem to have a private life worth talking about. So his being a monomaniac of all things Ferrari is a real big help. With that …"

Another page, lists of names.

"With that, I began the search in earnest. He canceled his paper subscription to ENZO a month before disappearing. This is a list of requests for online subscriptions to ENZO starting from the day he disappeared. There are 82 requests, from all over the world."

Another list. "These are new avatars on the forums, or rather people who have never posted before, starting from the day of his disappearance. Three names began to post regularly, showing a fanatical interest in the topics he was rabid about, starting from the week after he disappeared. Anselmo, Drake, Cavalier. The IP was different, but a word frequency analysis gave an 85% probability of it being the same author. All eventually traceable back to the same IP, though I had to work a little to find that out." Elle frowned, shook her head. "Anselmo is Enzo Ferrari's middle name. His nickname was 'il Drake' and he was made a Knight by the Italian government, a *Cavaliere*. Those three avatars shared the same IP."

"Wow." Bennett sat back. "That's amazing. I think with the IP alone we could find him."

"Oh." Elle gave a secretive little smile. "I told

you. I've already found him! The IP is traceable back to Bali. I'll bet he wanted to start his new life immediately. I can't imagine him waiting too long. If he has a lot of money stashed away, he'll want his Ferrari immediately. As a matter of fact," she looked at Bennett with sorrow, "I can well imagine that buying himself a Ferrari was what prompted him to turn treasonous. Though I cannot imagine committing treason and causing people to be murdered for a *car*."

Bennett had known people to kill for an imagined slight. For pride, for a fucking cigarette. A car — a Ferrari no less — was incentive enough for some. You'd have to be a psychopath, of course, but plenty of those around.

Elle pointed at the screen. "So the nearest dealership is in Jakarta. There's a waiting list of about two months so I imagined he'd want to get his name in fast. And sure enough, a week after disappearing, we have a Mr. Colby Sanders ordering a Ferrari with all the trimmings from the Jakarta dealership. It cost £250,000."

A security cam image came up on her monitor and *goddamn*! There he was! Arthur Kudlow. He'd shaved his head and grown a brand-new moth-eaten ginger goatee and he had a reddish tan, but there he was, shaking hands with someone who was presumably the owner of the dealership, wearing a shit-eating grin. Ordering his dream car, the car that had so far cost five lives and would cost many more. Not that Arthur gave a flying fuck. He was getting his shiny red wet dream.

Bennett turned his head. The reason no more people would die and that Arthur would soon be in prison was sitting right next to him, the smartest and most beautiful woman he'd ever known. Who'd found one man among the seven and a half billion people in the world. A man who'd wiped all traces of his previous self, and who'd had an army of the best and brightest looking for him.

"What?" Elle had said something and he wasn't listening.

"I said," she repeated patiently, "he tried to change his appearance, but facial recognition doesn't pay attention to hair on the head or facial hair. Facial recognition is based on distance between pupils, the shape of ears, the distance between the nose and mouth. It's him. Definitely. So with that knowledge, I looked at the purchase order and came up with his address, which corresponds to a luxury villa ten miles from Denpasar, the capital of Bali. I hacked into the villa's security cameras and sure enough —"

Another photograph, this time of a naked Arthur Ludlow near an elaborately decorated sky-blue swimming pool.

They both stared. "Maybe I should have pixelated his genitals," she said finally, scrunching her nose in distaste.

"Two pixels," he answered. "That's all it would take. That man clearly needs a Ferrari as compensation for what Mother Nature didn't give him. Right. I need to call this in. Do you think you can —"

"Done." Elle gave him one of her satisfied smiles. "I put all the info in a file and I've already sent it to you. Look for a file called Finding Kudlow in your downloads."

He had his cell to his ear as he opened the file up with one hand. Sure enough, there it was. When his right-hand man, Stuart Forsyth, answered, he said, "Stu. We found Ludlow. Or rather —" he shot a sideways glance at Elle. "Someone very bright found him for us. I'm sending you the entire file, plus recent photos. One of which is pretty nasty, will make your eyes bleed. But you're tough. You survived Hell Week with me, so you can take it. Make sure Kudlow's former employer is informed. And call off our dogs and give them a couple of days off. They've been working on this nonstop."

"You wrapping up the current job too, boss?" Stuart asked.

Bennett had a moment of panic. Wrapping this job up? God *no*! Because then he'd have to tip Elle back into the world and he loved it here with her, in their deluxe den. "No!" he said, then tempered his voice when Elle looked at him in surprise. He cleared his throat. "No, ah. Still the same contract. We'll be in touch. Forward that file."

Stuart waited a beat, two. He was no dummy. "Oh-kay boss. Keep it loose." He disconnected, leaving Bennett holding his cell with a clammy hand. He'd broken out in a sweat at the thought of leaving

Elle.

Keep it loose. Yeah.

Elle smiled at him. It wasn't a sweet gentle girly smile. It was a smile full of challenge. *Throw me something really hard*, it said. The air around her vibrated. Bennett had something hard for her. Real hard.

Eight

They'd been working their way toward this from the beginning.

Well, maybe not the *beginning* beginning, when he'd knocked her out and kidnapped her, but soon after she woke up. Elle had never felt so alive in her life as next to this strong savvy man, who was both a modern guy and at the same time made her feel like Cave Girl 1.0. The unwoke model.

He put a big hand behind her head and brought her face toward his. He didn't need to exert pressure in any way, she came willingly. As a matter of fact, she'd die if she didn't get a chance to come closer to him, touch him all over.

Before, he'd kissed her, but now she kissed him. It was absolutely irresistible, like magnetic filings. Like there was a vast tilting of the earth that tilted her right into his arms and nothing else was possible.

Only this.

While kissing, Bennett reached and lifted her onto his lap as if she weighed nothing. She straddled him, feeling the strength of his thighs under her, feeling the strength of his shoulders against her arms.

She had sensory overload, as if kissing Bennett while holding him at the same time was simply too much. Her head pulled back and she watched his face while her body was going haywire.

They'd kissed, sure, but it had been fleeting. Now, it seemed that all of her was touching him. Her thighs were opened wide over his own thick thighs and a big hand against her back, between her shoulder blades, held her chest against his. She felt like melting, held together by his arms around her.

Bennett didn't look like he was melting. Every muscle she could touch felt tense and hard. His face, too, was tense, a little pale. As if there were some strong emotion there. His eyes, slightly narrowed, were studying her.

What was he seeing?

Not the normal Elle, nope. The normal Elle was always detached, a little remote, even when in the arms of a man. Well, she'd never been in the arms of a man like Bennett before and she didn't feel detached. She felt attached, if anything. Tied to Bennett by some kind of supernatural glue. She couldn't pull away from him if she tried. And she didn't want to try.

His eyes alone were holding her. Dark and penetrating, as if he could see right into her. Normally, Elle thought of herself as a fairly complicated person. But right now? Right now she was reduced to the essentials, skin holding together raging hormones. She was boiling inside, an intense heat that had nothing to do with the temperature in the room.

Bennett noticed it. Of course he did. He noticed everything. His dark eyes roamed her face, watching her carefully. The hand against her back, holding her to him, dropped to the hem of her top and slid under it. His eyes narrowed even further as her eyes drooped and as she became even pinker. She could actually feel the rush of blood to her face. And to the area between her legs. The very first time she'd felt that happen. It was like a sunburst in her core. She drew in a long, shaky breath.

So this, *this* was desire. Not a mild itch but a raging storm penetrating every cell. She'd read about it and thought it was like a literary convention, but no. It was real. This was real. And it was amazing.

Her body doing its own bidding, not hers. It sort of felt like even if she, as a person, didn't want Bennett, her body sure did. Her body, separate from her.

It was lucky then, that she wanted Bennett, too.

She wasn't the only one with a rush of blood. Bennett had a rush of blood to his groin, too. She was sitting practically right on top of him and could feel everything. He was huge, which would have worried her if all the worry receptors hadn't been burned right out of her brain.

Elle firmly believed in equality of the sexes. He was feeling her under her top so she would, too. She ran her hands over his broad back down to the hem of his sweater and slipped both hands underneath the fine wool.

Oh God. Warm skin, hard muscle. She'd never felt anything like it. There was electricity in touching him, like touching something primal, a force of nature. His skin was a magnet for her hands.

He was kissing her neck which — surprise! — was an erogenous zone. When he gently dragged his teeth along a sensitive part of her neck she curled her nails into his back as heat blossomed inside her. His penis grew. He bit her again and she moaned and clutched his back and his penis grew even longer, harder.

Their bodies were engaged in a little erotic dance.

She explored the broad expanse of his back, feeling each muscle distinctly. Then her fingers encountered hard tissue. Scar tissue, round. A bullet scar, where he'd been shot. She touched it lightly then lifted her head as he lifted his.

They stared at each other. A muscle twitched in his jaw.

Elle was a storm of emotions, all raw and real. This was as real as it got. He'd been shot and survived. He could have died. He'd put his life on the line and had paid the price, but he was still here.

If he had died, she'd never have known this. In her almost thirty years on this earth she'd never felt this burning desire before and probably never would have if not for Bennett.

She fingered his scar. "You survived," she whispered.

He nodded, a short jerk of his head.

"I'm so glad you did." The words came out of her without volition, straight from the depths of her heart.

She was so glad he was alive and right here in her arms.

Bennett closed his eyes and kissed her again. He kissed her with his whole body and she broke out in goose bumps. It was so intense she could hardly breathe, could barely move except to wriggle to get even closer to him.

His hand pressed down against her back while moving his hips forward and suddenly she was riding him. The folds of her sex opened up and there he was, separated from her flesh by layers of cloth, hers and his.

She moved, riding him, and felt him shudder.

Oh, wow. She made this strong man, the strongest man she'd ever met, shudder and shake. This was power, power unlike any she'd ever known before. She was the most powerful woman in the world.

Let's test this, she thought, and nipped his lower lip. He jolted, kissed her harder. A twist of her hips and she slid along his penis and he moaned into her mouth, tightening his arms around her. Digging her hands into his back she slid over him again while heat erupted everywhere she touched him.

Again and again, and suddenly he surged up with her in his arms and carried them into her bedroom. It felt like flying, like she had suddenly been freed from the bonds of the earth. Better than flying because he was still kissing her. Dimly, Elle wondered how he didn't bump into the furniture but he didn't. In an instant, Bennett was laying her down on the bed. For a moment, just a moment, she felt cold because he wasn't holding her any more. But then he was stripping and she didn't feel cold at all. If anything, the heat notched up several degrees.

He crossed his arms and pulled his sweater up and over his head, tossing it onto a chair. The instant it hit the chair, he removed his boots and socks, shucked his jeans and briefs and there he was. The most beautiful man she'd ever seen.

She'd seen him in an old tattered wife beater and shorts but naked, he was something else. Long and lean, muscles so defined he could have been a living anatomy atlas. Raised veins were visible all over his body. Elle had been around powerful men all her life. Her father was one of the richest men in the world. Her step-father was CEO of a large corporation. She'd worked with Nobel prize winners and MacArthur 'Genius' Grant recipients. But Bennett was another type of power altogether, a primitive form of power but the real deal. When the world went to shit, the other men would lose their power.

Bennett would never lose his. Only death could take it away.

He'd skirted death, many times.

He stood before her, naked, almost in a fighting stance. His chest was heaving as if he'd run miles to her.

They stared at each other. Wordlessly, Elle stripped. She sat up, pulled off the yoga top, unhooked her bra, slid her silky yoga pants and lace panties down her legs. Bennett followed every move she made, without moving a muscle himself.

When she was naked, Elle lay back down and held her arms up. "Come to me, Bennett," she whispered.

It was as if her words freed him from shackles. In a step he was at the bedside and a second later he was lying on top of her. They both shuddered. It was such a relief feeling him on her, his weight pushing her down. As if without that weight she'd just float up and away.

She needed that weight. She needed him.

Bennett placed a forearm on the bed next to her head and lifted his torso. His other hand covered her mound. As if she needed more heat there. It felt like a furnace, on fire. Long fingers covered her, reached the opening of her sex, stroked her there.

Bennett looked down at the picture they made, then lifted his eyes to hers. "You're so goddamned beautiful." His voice was hoarse, as if he hadn't spoken in years. "I don't know where to start."

That made her smile. "You'll figure it out."

His eyes never left hers. "I will."

Fingers touched her, entered her. An electric bolt of pleasure speared through her.

Bennett closed his eyes then opened them again. "You're wet."

She smiled. "I am."

His finger slid in and out of her and this time she closed her eyes. A sigh left her mouth. Without thought, her hips lifted.

"You're ready."

Her eyes opened at that. The breath in her lungs was hot and she couldn't speak. She nodded because, yes, she was ready. It usually took a lot of foreplay for her to be ready but she was ready *now*. So ready it shocked her. He'd barely touched her and she was ready to come. It felt like she'd been preparing for this moment her whole life.

Bennett shifted his hips and entered her in one hard shocking stroke. He stopped, propped on his forearms, hands cupping her head. "God," he muttered. "Sorry."

Elle shut her eyes, all her attention concentrated inward, particularly to where he filled her completely. It was almost, but not quite, painful. On the knife's edge between pain and blinding pleasure.

Don't apologize, she wanted to say but didn't have the breath to do it. She arched, spread her legs and he sank a little deeper into her and it wasn't that fine line between pain and blinding pleasure any more. It was just blinding pleasure.

With a small cry, she fell into orgasm, clenching around him tightly and oh God, he started coming too. Impossibly intense spurts that went on forever. Through it all, he kissed her, holding her head tightly, and pressed into her as hard as he could, drowning his moans in her mouth.

It went on forever. Time just stopped while her body went into overdrive as she clutched him as hard as she could, gripping him with her arms and legs. She would explode if she didn't hold onto him hard.

He started moving in her, hard jabs that didn't hurt because she was so wet all she felt was the heat, the sensation of being filled.

Finally the tension left her. Her arms collapsed by her sides, her legs opened. She felt completely lax, wiped out, muscles like rubber. No thoughts in her head at all. Her brain had taken a hike while her body took over. Pleasure at that level was almost frightening.

He lifted his mouth from hers and his lips were red and slightly swollen. Who knew what she looked like? She was probably the very picture of wanton abandon, arms and legs out, Bennett on top of her, still *in* her.

"Whoa." He shook his head. He wasn't smiling but there was a lightness to his expression. "I'm really sorry. I'm not usually that trigger happy." He flicked the small dent in her chin. "It's because you're so amazingly desirable."

Elle didn't have the energy to roll her eyes but she smiled faintly. "So it's all my fault?"

He heaved a huge sigh. She could feel that massive chest expand. "No, honey, it's mine." Now he smiled. "It'll be better next time."

Any better and she'd be dead, but she didn't say that. "I don't know. It was pretty good. I'd give you an A."

He grinned. "Yeah?"

He pulled away then slid back into her. Somehow he was still hard. Elle had no idea men could do that. "An A?"

Another slide into her and her vagina actually fluttered.

"Okay," she sighed as her arms came around him again. "An A+."

The next morning, Bennett lifted his head from the pillow then dropped it again. He was covered in sweat, exhausted and revved, both at the same time. Like he could go three or four hundred rounds in the ring with a sparring partner, if he could just stand up. He turned his head on the pillow to look at her. She was staring at the ceiling. Thank God she had a smile on her face.

"All of this is so out of bounds," he said. But he was smiling. "I should so fire my ass."

She looked at him out of the corner of her eyes, not moving her head. "Yeah?" she said lazily. "Why?"

Bennett lifted himself up onto his elbow and looked down at her, totally delighted at what he saw. He put his face against her neck and inhaled. She

smelled so good. Some floral scent plus an overlay of
sex. Best smell in the world. "Told you. No fraternizing with principals."

She ran a hand lazily over his back, stopping, as
she'd done before, at the bullet scar. "I'd call what we
did all night a little more than fraternization. Maybe
you *should* fire you."

He kissed her shoulder. "But I'd have to get out
of bed to fire my ass."

She sighed. Smoothed her hand down his back,
over his ass. Clutched it. "And a very fine ass it is,
too."

He laughed as he went from semi-hard to raging
woodie. He shifted so he was lying on top of her, taking the weight of his torso on his arms. His hands
were in her hair, holding her head still. Shiny blue-
black hair fell over his fingers.

"I keep expecting your hair to be cold, it's so
black. But it's not. It's warm."

Luckily she didn't comment on his stupid remark.

"It's an amazing color. And your eyes ... Jesus.
You have that whole Snow White thing going on."

"I inherited my coloring from my mom. She was a
real beauty in her day. Still is very beautiful."

He wondered whether she'd gotten her smarts
from her mom or from Ricks. And thanked the stars
above again that she hadn't inherited his looks.

"Why'd your dad leave her?"

Her mouth quirked. "I think he truly loved her.
More than any of his other wives. It's just that mom

made the fatal mistake of aging, so, like he does with his cars and houses, he turned her in for a newer model. Didn't work though. His wives just kept getting younger and younger and stupider and stupider. My dad is pretty good at money but not so good at being human."

Bennett ran his finger down the side of her face, admiring the fine facial bones. This was a woman who would be beautiful and turning heads at eighty. "He's a moron."

She laughed. "Pretty much. And he lost out in the end. My mom cried for years after he left us and then she met my step dad, Matthew Castle. He adopted me and I love him like a father. Certainly more than my own dad. Mom and Matt are wildly happy. My dad's last wife was Bulgarian with some gypsy blood in her. I heard she cursed him before leaving. They say he was really spooked."

Bennett had very little bandwidth to pity Clifford Ricks when he had the daughter Ricks had ignored under him. This wasn't a woman you ignored. So soft, so bright. A lot of tart snark came from a mouth that was amazingly soft.

He wanted to keep talking to her but his body had other plans. He shifted so he was completely on top of her, realizing that they were again in the missionary position after being in the missionary position all night. He couldn't even wrap his head around experimenting when all he wanted was to mount her, in as primitive a fashion as possible.

Going missionary had its advantages. God yes. He could watch her beautiful face and touch her all over while fucking her. What was better than that?

He was revved — was she? He bent to kiss her neck, knowing exactly the spots that excited her. He was going to get a fucking PhD in Elle Castle. He was going to know everything about her, inside and out, before he was done.

And he was going to take his time about it, too because being with her was just the greatest.

So he was going to go over his lesson notes. A lick of her ear that made her shudder, check. A light bite behind her ear that made her sigh, check. Sliding his fingers into her between her legs, feeling her slowly become wet, oh yeah. Check check check.

"Bennett," she sighed.

"Right here," he whispered into her ear then licked it.

She was ready and he felt like he'd been born ready. He entered her and she was so tight and soft he felt like his head would explode. No exploding right away, though, no. He'd done that twice last night and goddamn it, he was known for his self control. He could last a long time, except with Elle, the one woman he wanted to please above all others.

She hadn't complained, but still.

He held himself inside her because, well, it felt so goddamned good. Already he could feel tension along his spine but he wasn't going to come in an instant. Nope.

He pulled out, wanting this to be leisurely, but immediately moved back in. Out. In. Out. In.

His skin felt too tight, and electricity crackled in the air.

In.

Out.

He started shaking. Elle's head pushed back against the pillows, long white throat exposed and as she gave a sharp cry, she tightened around him in sharp contractions.

In. Out. In. Out. Inoutinoutinout …

Bennett put his face against her head and muffled his shout in the pillow. He was pouring sweat, his hair, his groin wet with it.

He closed his eyes and stifled a groan as he climaxed. He was definitely going to get over this initial phase of uncontrollable excitement. Definitely. Though who knew when?

Elle gave a little laugh and trailed her fingers lazily up his back. Stopping, as always, at his bullet scar.

He barely had the energy to keep his eyes open.

"That was funny?" he mumbled.

"No." She trailed her hand back down his back and cupped his ass. "I was trying to think of a higher grade than A+." She turned her head and smiled at him. "So what are we going to do today?"

"Never mess with a winning formula. How about this? I go beat a punching bag to death while you watch. You go swimming while I watch. I feed you. Then I give you a really hard problem to solve and you solve it. I feed you then I take you to bed." He smiled at her. "How does that sound as a plan?"

"Perfect," she sighed.

Nine

It *was* a perfect day, particularly the part where she got to watch him working out half naked. Hmmm. This time she didn't have to pretend. She simply sat down and watched him, watched that wonderful body with all those muscles working in perfect harmony brutally beat the shit out of a bag.

He knew she was watching him, but after a minute or two, she also sensed that he'd forgotten her, forgotten the world and was focused like a laser beam on wreaking havoc on a sand-filled leather bag.

She knew he was focused because she recognized that expression, that intensity, that utter concentration. It was what she had when she was immersed in a task. When the world disappeared and you were one with the swim, or the code or the theorem. Not many people had that gift but she had it and Bennett had it in spades.

In the apartment he was a perfectly affable companion. Easy-going and fun. Like a big Labrador or German Shephard, friendly and eager to please. She knew it was because he felt they were safe in the apartment itself, barring a bomb dropped from a plane taking out an entire wing of Sparrow Square.

But the instant the apartment's door closed behind them, he morphed into a Rottweiler.

Though he knew she was wiping their faces from the system when they walked down the corridors and in the elevator going down to the pool, he was completely outwardly focused, his attention on a 360° circle around them. If the Art Deco wall sconces suddenly took flight and turned into drones, if ravenous Predator-like aliens dropped from the ceiling, if they found bad guys around corners, she had no doubt he'd be ready and with a plan.

He relaxed a little — just a little — when she was in the pool, partly because he repeated yesterday's trick of tying the handles of the only access doors with zip ties, watching her with his dark eyes as she swam her laps.

She was perfectly safe. If anything, the danger came from within her.

Her body felt ... different. Well, she'd had more and better sex last night and this morning than ... ever, really. Intimate muscles were sore and she was glad of warm water and exercise. She was intensely aware of her body those first few laps and was surprised at the effort it took to coordinate her limbs. She'd swum daily since she was seven. Her body took over the instant she hit the water.

But today ... well, it took some time to find her rhythm, and she was very aware of Bennett, sitting on a deck chair, watching her, focused on her. His attention felt like something tangible, like a hand touching her.

He somehow knew when she started to flag, and when she popped her head up, pushing up her swim goggles, there he was with a huge hand held down to help her out.

He lifted her out of the pool with no effort whatsoever and held out a towel for her, wrapping it around her. There was no one else around so she allowed herself to be wrapped like a mummy and stepped into his arms, leaning her head against his shoulder. It was the most extraordinary feeling, as if he could lend her his strength. Or rather, he placed his strength — all those long, lean muscles — at her service.

He didn't kiss her, though. His vigilance was unceasing. He held her tightly, but his head moved and he kept an eye on the doors.

"How about you dry off upstairs?" he asked. She felt the rumble of his voice in his chest, ear against him.

She blinked. "Sure." And only on the trip back up to the apartment did she realize he wanted to minimize the time outside and, at least in theory, exposed.

Once they were in the apartment, he relaxed that iron vigilance. He dropped a kiss on the top of her head. "Why don't you go shower and lunch will be ready when you come out?"

She smiled up at him. "Cooked or catered?"

"Catered. I ordered and I hope I got your tastes

right. Tonight we'll order in again, whatever you want. But I'll cook you something special tomorrow."

A handsome man cooking for her. Didn't get much better than that. "Sounds good. And this afternoon you'll give me a problem to solve?"

"Oh, yeah," he said softly. "Count on it."

Lunch was exactly to her tastes. French onion soup and a big fish platter to share, with fries and garlic mayonnaise. She ate everything and all but licked her fingers. "What are you going to cook for me tomorrow?"

"Something healthy. You have the tastes of a twelve-year-old boy. I think you could probably live off pizza and burgers."

"I could," she answered. "I have."

"You need a keeper," he grumbled and her head shot up at that. Their eyes met with an almost magnetic clank. Electricity crackled in the air, a nearly visible arc running between them. Elle was surprised the fine hairs on her forearm didn't rise. A band tightened around her chest and she forgot to breathe for a moment.

He too looked electrified, dark eyes so intense they seemed to shine.

She couldn't look at him, couldn't look away from him, was utterly paralyzed. The words *are you applying for the job?* lingered on her lips and she had to bite them to keep the question in.

Because, well.

Having Bennett Cameron as a keeper didn't

sound bad, didn't sound bad at all. He was a really good keeper.

Elle traveled the world and she traveled alone, fully aware that a single woman was prey in most parts of the globe. So she was always alert and dedicated a lot of attention to her surroundings, and as a consequence was rarely completely relaxed when outside in the world. Feeling tense was a natural state.

She hadn't even realized it until now.

Being with Bennett was like sinking into a warm bath. No need to feel any apprehension at all. She could sink right into her own mind and not pay any attention to the outside world, because, well, he was there. And nobody in his right mind would dare hurt her with Bennett at her side.

It was exhilarating. Addictive. Extremely retro, probably primitive, but an amazing feeling.

And on top of it, Bennett wasn't in any way a bully or overbearing. She felt totally free to do as she pleased as long as it didn't affect her safety. Though it did look like he was trying to nudge her toward a healthier diet. Which was okay, because when she was taken up with work, which was always, takeout was the default option.

You need a keeper.

Bennett was the first to break eye contact. Elle could feel the rush of blood to her cheeks and cursed her fair skin. Her mortification must be clear to read on her face. Stop-light red was a hard color to ignore.

It was lucky she'd never been so attracted to a

man before. Not even close. The one time she'd felt this amount of blood rush to her head, it had been because a student pointed out a fallacy in a formula on the screen during a lesson.

When Bennett turned his head away, it was like she'd been unplugged. A huge source of energy suddenly cut off.

He rose, cleared the dishes, put them in the sink. Well, he'd made her feel unsettled. As payback, he *should* clear the table. Only fair.

Speaking of which …

"You owe me a problem," she called out to his broad back, big hands handling the delicate porcelain plates with care.

When he turned back to her, he had a half smile on his face. "I do." The smile became complete. "It's a doozy. Let's see you think your way out of this one. It's going to be fun to watch."

Bennett handed her the thorniest of thorny problems his company was dealing with. He'd hired fifteen new operatives — ten men, five women — for this single operation. All of them were assigned to round-the-clock surveillance. Another twenty were on SIGINT — signals intelligence. Which was a fancy way of saying they manned surveillance stations 24/7 monitoring cellphones, computers, landlines, security video footage.

The two of them were sitting at the big desk that had been cleared and was now their workstation. It was so weird. This was day two of their collaboration and already Bennett felt comfortable. Elle sat with her hands in her lap, laptop open, fully turned to him, ready to hear what she called 'the parameters' of the problem.

The parameters of the problem were that it was shitty.

"This is a private company so there are no national security implications. I am going to consider you a temporary subcontractor of my company so there are no issues with giving you full access to intel."

She cocked her head. "A temporary subcontractor? How much will you pay me for my services?"

He smiled. "Name your price." His company's contract was huge. They could afford more or less whatever she wanted.

"Tickets to Les Mis."

"What?"

"You heard me. They are almost impossible to find, particularly in London. So I want two tickets to my favorite musical when this is over and I want you to accompany me."

Oh man. He'd never seen Les Mis. *Fuck* yeah. "Done. And dinner first."

"Okay." She lifted her hands and placed them

over her keyboard. His hands went to his own laptop next to hers and he transferred a big file. A really big file. While it was loading, he gave her an oral brief. "It's a big tech company. Sydotek."

She whistled. "That is big."

Bennett nodded. "They are working on something that has huge implications, could revolutionize computing and could potentially be worth billions."

Elle nodded, intelligent face sober. "Probably something to do with the next step toward quantum computers."

Bingo.

He stared. "How did you — never mind." All he had to do was look at that bright face and those intelligent eyes to figure out how she'd figured it out. This was her domain. He felt hope stirring. Maybe she really would be able to help them.

She sighed. "If that's it, you didn't overstate it. It would be revolutionary and worth billions. Someone is stealing the research."

This time he didn't stare, but he did smile. "Four hundred years ago you would have been burned at the stake."

She didn't smile back.

He glanced at her monitor. His file had already loaded which meant her computer was amazingly powerful. He knew for a fact that the file took even the most powerful commercially-available computers at least a quarter of an hour to load. Hers just sipped it right up like a fine wine.

"Ok. What you have in that file is an immense amount of data, including footage. I don't know how you can get through it in less than a week but I'm giving it to you anyway. The head office discovered proprietary research popping up in a state lab in China. This lab is following Sydotek's developments step by step. Someone is feeding them intel from the inside."

"That's very bad," she said. "How many people work in the Sydotek lab?"

"It's a big one, but only five people have access to all the research and would understand it. Four men and a woman. All PhDs, all super smart, all seemingly innocent, all going about their daily business normally, no one with unexplained sums of money in the bank. The company is terrified of accusing the wrong researcher. They are all rainmakers, all essential. The company doesn't want to make a mistake. But on the other hand, as the research gets closer and closer to a working model, they also don't want the work to appear in China first. It would be a huge blow."

"Understandable," she murmured.

Her index finger with the blue fingernail polish stroked the side of her laptop. Ordinarily Bennett hated that crap — black lipstick, dark fingernail polish. But on her it looked really good, highlighting the fine pale skin of her hands. He shook his head. How could he be thinking of fingernail polish right now? The Sydotek contract was worth well over five million dollars, they were nowhere near wrapping it up and here he was mooning over the paint on her fingernails.

"So what is in that mega file?"

"A ton of stuff," Bennett said with a touch of exasperation in his voice. They'd spent countless man-hours collecting it and had fuckall to show for it. "I've got a lot of men and women combing through their work emails, following them, on round-the-clock surveillance, going through bank statements. One of our guys even went dumpster diving because he thought one of the researchers threw something suspicious away. It was cat litter and my guy stank of cat piss for days afterward. So you'll have to sort things out for yourself. I don't want to give you any guidance because, by definition, we have missed something. You might catch it if I don't bias you."

"Okay." She bent forward a little, studying what he'd sent. A lot of material organized as best he could. Her eyes scanned the screen like a metronome.

"It'll take you a while to familiarize yourself with the material, and how it's structured," he said uneasily. He'd thrown a massive knotty lump of data at her. It was really unfair. "Listen." He shifted in his chair. "Maybe we should try another issue …"

Elle flicked her fingers at him, never taking her eyes from the screen. "Don't you have work to do?"

Well, yes, yes he did. A lot of it actually. Admin stuff, mostly. New equipment to assess and order. Bonuses. Fielding job applications. There was a lot to catch up on. It was why he rarely accepted close protection assignments, because you dropped out of the world for the duration of the assignment and he had a big company to run.

So he did what Elle did — he disappeared into his computer. Not quite as thoroughly as she did, though. Every once in a while he'd look up from his screen to glance at her. Just to reassure himself that aliens hadn't abducted her while he dealt with the bids on a new corporate jet.

But she wasn't looking up to check up on him, nope. She was so immersed in what she was doing that she put him to shame. Damn it, he ran a billion-dollar business, he should be as focused as she was.

Her focus was actually alarming.

After a while, he realized that she wasn't stopping for anything. He got up to put a cup of tea next to her elbow. He'd stocked up on a wide variety and prepared his favorite black tea for her, Lady Grey. She sipped absent-mindedly. At 4 pm he ordered scones and a fruit platter for both of them. She ate every bite without taking her eyes from the monitor. It was amazing.

Bennett dug deep into work, printing off specs and comparing them. It would be his third corporate jet and he needed to balance an ability to fly at least twenty people in comfort over long distances with fuel efficiency. He consulted with his chief pilots in chat function and was close to a decision when Elle made a sound.

His head whipped up. It was the first sound she'd

made in five hours. The sky outside had turned dark gray.

She was sitting back, arching her spine to work the kinks out. "You okay?" he asked. "Listen, quit for the day. You can pick it up tomorrow, when you've rested. I don't want —"

"I got it," she said, smiling at him.

He stared at her. She was just so beautiful. He hadn't looked at her in over two hours and he was struck anew by just how gorgeous she was. "Got what?" he asked stupidly.

She looked at him oddly. "The culprit." Elle shook her head. "Remember? The physicist who is selling intel?"

"You *got* him?" Bennett's eyes widened. His best minds had been at work for almost a month on this. "You sure?"

She didn't take offense. She was too smart for that. "I'm sure. And I got *her,* not him."

"The woman?" Bennett felt like he'd just woken up, was just catching up to her. He scooted his chair closer to hers. "Show me."

Elle pulled up something that looked weird. Graphics of some type. Twisted cubes with bright lines running through them, bottom to top. Five of them. They were beautiful in an abstract sort of way.

Elle clicked a button and the image of the cubes sharpened until they looked like CGI. They were intriguing and even attractive, like a form of art. But they had no meaning for him.

"What am I looking at?"

Elle clicked another button and those handsome tantalizingly enigmatic cubes did a little dance. Originally, they had been in a row, the same size, taking up the width of Elle's monitor. Suddenly, the first one expanded in size and the other four disappeared. Then they all were lined up again, and the second one loomed in the foreground while the other four disappeared. Then the third, the fourth and the fifth.

Then the process started all over again.

It was mesmerizing, almost beautiful.

"Bennett?"

It was almost impossible to pull his eyes away. "Huh?"

She blew out a breath. "Pay attention. It's important."

He was being chastised. That was okay. It was Elle chastising him. "Yes, ma'am." He repeated his question. "What am I looking at here?"

She tapped the screen with a fingernail. "You're looking at a representation of Minkowski space. Minkowski space is where three dimensional Euclidean space is united with time into a four-dimensional manifold."

Bennett's mouth opened and closed. He grunted.

"In simpler terms, what we're looking at is a graphic representation of the three dimensions of space together with the fourth dimension, time."

Bennett grunted again.

Elle's fingernail slowly rose from the bottom of

the twisted cube to the top. Inside the cube was a brightly lit line. "This line is a series of dots. Each dot represents something important about the scientist's life. The dots form a line which is the timeline. So from bottom to top is a representation of the scientist's life, over a period of time. You'll notice that the line becomes thicker at a certain point."

Bennett peered closely. "Yep." That was safe to say. It did become thicker about a quarter of the way up.

"The line is a condensation of data. Where it becomes thicker is where your company started observing and there's more data. From before that point in time, I put together what data I could on the basis of the information you sent. After which, I did data analysis on your five candidates. I know your guys have already studied the scientists' bank accounts and spending habits to see if they have extra money that is unaccounted for."

Bennett nodded. Yeah, his team of analysts had gone over the five physicists' records with a fine-tooth comb. "They didn't find much. Certainly nothing definitive."

She nodded back. "I knew your guys would be good, so I didn't go over that ground. It would have been a waste of time. So I took a different tack, taking it as a given that if one of these five is selling info, their habits would change, even while being stealthy. It would be more an unconscious thing. I think anyone smart enough to work on a quantum computer is smart enough to cover their tracks. They won't be suddenly buying real estate, at least not in the US, or buying mink coats or a Porsche or suddenly spending wildly. They would be too smart for that. But I also felt that whoever it is would be in a state of … excitement, for lack of a better word. He or she wouldn't spend wildly, but money would have a different meaning for them. They are each probably pulling down at least 300k per year, but if someone is selling secrets, his or her income has suddenly gone up tenfold, at least. That changes the way they deal with daily life. Does this make sense so far?"

Bennett put his hand on her shoulder. As always, he felt a little electric shock, like she was a source of energy. This beautiful woman practically hummed with it. "Yeah. Makes sense."

"So these Minkowski cubes represent the five scientists' lives starting from six months before your starting point. I took as many elements as I could — use of utilities, time spent watching streaming TV channels, evenings out, books ordered and read, meal takeouts — and weighted them. Most people's lives are like Brownian movement at a constant temperature. Lots of movement but in the aggregate nothing changes. So look at the five lives over time."

She tapped the keyboard and the cubes sliced themselves horizontally and curled up, giving a clearer view of the lines which he could now see become discrete points of light.

Bennett looked at the cubes again, beginning to

understand them. Each cube's bright line forged a different path but somehow they were similar as they snaked their way up the cube from the bottom, sort of like five heartbeats of a hospital monitor only vertical instead of horizontal. There were changes for all of them but the patterns repeated over and over. Each pattern was slightly different, but each pattern for each person remained the same.

"So their lives are fairly regular," Elle said as they watched January turn into February and March. Then the spring and summer. "In summer everyone's life sort of picks up." Like watching a patient's heart rate increase.

"Here." Elle's voice was calm but Bennett sat up straight. In one of the cubes the line of light went haywire. He checked the timeline and it was when secrets began leaking. Leaning forward to check the monitor, he heard Elle say, "Don't bother checking. It's the woman, Dr. Haverson."

"Whoa." Bennett leaned back. "We checked carefully. Her bank balance didn't change. She didn't make any major purchases."

"No. She has a PhD in particle physics and a masters in electrical engineering. She's not a dummy. But her life changed enormously and the graph bears it out. Everything she did, she did more of. Speeded up. Joined a gym. Joined two gyms, actually, but rarely went to either one. Went to more movies, went out to dinner more often, made more phone calls, used more internet bandwidth. I peeked. She used it mainly to scout foreign real estate. So she didn't spend money but she was a little … feverish because she knew she had a lot of it. And more was coming."

He pointed to wild zigzags, while the other scientists' data remained fairly smooth. "What's this?"

"Well, that's my point. Look, your scientists are top tier. They get paid generous salaries and they all drive late model luxury vehicles. Which have wireless tire pressure monitors. I hacked into them. Four drove the same amount of miles with a margin of about 10%. Her miles went up and up and up. I didn't follow where she went. I think it just shows that her Brownian movement speeded up. Someone applied heat. A lot of it."

"Wow." Bennett leaned forward and kissed her cheek, velvety and smelling of some kind of herb, something maybe you'd put in a tea cup. Or take a bath in. And maybe there was some fairy dust mingled in, because God knew the woman was magic. "Now that we know who it is, we can dig more." Her mouth tightened and she looked away from him. "What?"

"Well," she said sheepishly, "since I was there, I did a little digging myself."

He smiled. Sure she had. "What did you find?"

She pointed. "This."

Bennett stared at a screen full of hieroglyphs, numbers and letters, completely incomprehensible. Before he could say anything, the screen started moving, scrolling down. And sure enough, comprehensible words showed up.

He leaned closer. An email exchange but nothing like email exchanges organized by Gmail or Outlook or any of the other email programs. This was just plaintext, like text messages on a phone.

Maybe they were. "Are these email or text messages?"

"Email. But we're in the dark web and they aren't organized."

Bennett didn't navigate the dark web swamp very often. The dark web was mostly made up of overlay exchanges — unregulated, unseen, unknown. Bennett was usually okay with computers, though nothing like at Elle's level. His things were weaponry and close protection and security issues. The dark web was mainly foreign terrain for him. He studied the screen carefully then sat back. "It's messages between 123 and MF. Do we know who they are?"

"It took some doing, but 123 is the Chief Officer of Cybersecurity of a People's Liberation Army unit in Shenzhen. And MF is our scientist. I don't know why she is characterized as MF."

"Wouldn't be motherfucker, would it?" Bennett mused, giving her a sidelong glance. "Sorry."

She frowned. "No, it wouldn't be that because she was the one who gave herself the handle, and she wouldn't call herself motherfucker. But the identifiers are not the interesting part. What the two parties say is what's interesting."

Bennett squinted and she enlarged the fonts.

"Thanks."

Elle nodded and waited for him to read the texts, scrolling down.

"Son of a bitch," he breathed when he'd reached the bottom. He'd just read an offer to sell the building blocks of his client's quantum computer to an agent of the Chinese military. MF understood quite well what she was doing, and who she was selling to. And the damage it would do to her company and, ultimately, her country.

Elle tapped the screen. "Look at the amounts."

Bennett ran his eyes over a ton of text and then bounced his fist lightly off the table. Son of a bitch. "That's ten million USD."

"Yes, it is. For the first transaction, the first transfer of knowledge. They didn't even know if what she would send them would be useful or viable. It was a shot in the dark. Ten million dollars is a lot of money for a shot in the dark."

"I guess it was worth it."

"Very definitely. And they might be like fishermen along the bank, casting lines. Ten-million-dollar lines. This one bit and it was a whopper."

"How many transactions so far?"

Elle dropped her hands to her lap and turned to him, her face sad. "There have been six transactions. The data transfers have been immense. And highly encrypted. Do you need for me to try to decipher?"

Bennett picked up her hands, held them in his, thumbs caressing the soft backs of hers. That crackling energy was a little diminished now. She'd worked in a fever of excitement, but the end product of all of that amazing work was finding a woman who was insanely greedy, able and willing to betray her colleagues, her company and her country for money. That was depressing enough to bring anyone's energy down.

He wouldn't have been capable of that kind of betrayal, for no matter what amount. There wasn't enough money in the world. And he knew, instinctively, she felt exactly the same.

He looked her in the eyes, those amazingly beautiful and expressive eyes.

"No, sweetheart, your work here is done. My client knows what's in those files. It's their proprietary information."

She pulled one hand away from Bennett's to touch a key, and a long alphanumeric list came up.

"Well, if they want the last element of proof, here it is."

He didn't even look at the screen, didn't take his eyes off her. "What is it?"

She sighed, looking even sadder. "It's a bank ID. No name, just a number that identifies the owner of the bank account. It's a bank in Panama. I think they can prove it's hers, once they have this number. Or they could just wait for her to connect with the bank and catch her that way. At any rate, I think you can tell your client it's over. They have their culprit and they can stop the leak of information."

"I will." Bennett gave a half smile. "That was good work, Elle. The best. Man, though, it's sad to see a scientist betray everything like this."

"Wait." She grinned, eyes wide, the light back in them. "I think I know a way to turn this around."

"Yeah?" Shit, there was no resisting her. It was great seeing her animated again, that look of sadness wiped from her face. Whatever it was, it was sure to be a good idea. That was the only kind she had. "Shoot."

"I think the Board of the company should let leak that one of their scientists, working on a top secret project, was inventing data. Then they fire her and put out word that she was let go because she was falsifying results. All the data she produced was bogus, worthless."

"Wow." Bennett whistled. "Brilliant. So the Chinese won't know whether to trust the data she sent or not."

"They will be angry. Those results would be very hard and insanely expensive to duplicate and they won't know whether it's a wild goose chase or not. They would just figure she was inventing data that was useless. Not only that." Elle's smile was wicked. "With that ID, the company can access the bank account, drain it completely, so the money is lost to the Chinese and to Dr. Haverson. Please ask them to donate a sum — say, ten percent of what they recover — to charity."

"Done. They are going to be really pleased. I

don't think they'll have any problems donating a percentage. They get their woman, get most of money the Chinese sent her, and throw serious doubt on what the Chinese have bought so far. It's perfect. Win-win. What's your charity?"

"I think … I think I'd like the money donated to Médecins sans Frontières. They do good work."

"They do indeed. So a very nice sum will be donated to the good doctors without borders. Now, can you send me the essence of this information in a form a company director who doesn't have a PhD in information technology and who probably inherited his shares from his father can understand, including the bank ID?"

"I can." She pressed a key. "And did."

No flies on this woman, no sir.

"And what do *you* want?" Bennett was feeling generous. She'd solved a big problem they'd been working on for weeks and weeks. Yesterday and today she'd done something invaluable. Apart from being amazing, she was worth her weight in gold. "Any ticket to any show, anywhere. A private meeting with the Pope. Anything, anything at all."

His hand stroked hers. He'd almost forgotten he was holding her hand, it felt so natural. How could anyone sit beside her and not hold her hand?

She cocked her head. "You know, right now, I can't think of anything I want that I don't already have. But while I ponder what you should give me, I think you should feed me. And make popcorn. And we can watch a movie on the couch and hold hands. Can we screen the new Mission Impossible? Or is it too early? It only came out last month."

Oh yeah. Something he could do for a woman who didn't want much for herself after handing him the professional equivalent of the moon.

Sparrow Square had an amazing inbuilt video system that screened first run movies. It was one of the many attractions of the place that prided itself on providing so much for the residents that they never had to leave. He'd get the Mission Impossible movie for her if he had to fly Tom Cruise himself here.

And anyway — it sounded like absolute heaven. Bennett couldn't imagine anything he wanted more than to celebrate with Elle in their cozy apartment, watching a kickass movie, eating popcorn, necking on the couch.

He kissed her. "Absolutely. Dinner and a movie coming right —"

The Skype call tone sounded, loud and jarring. What the fuck? Anything from work would be a call to his cell. Who the hell —

He checked his laptop monitor. Oh. The last thing he wanted to see. CLIFFORD RICKS IS CALLING.

Well, fuck. He was astonished to find that he was irritated with Ricks. What was wrong with the man?

Bennett and Elle were *just fine*. He didn't want to be interrupted by a client, particularly not this client. Bennett had spent his entire time as CEO of BMC by putting clients first. And second and third. But right now, he'd happily throw Ricks off a cliff to have his evening with Elle. An evening he was looking forward to more than any he could remember in a long, long time.

But. Duty was duty.

Hell.

Bennett clicked on the Skype app and the program that hid his location. The screen opened. It took him a moment to realize what he was seeing. The screen was all white, like the apparition of a ghost. Ricks's unkempt white hair was a messy cloud around his head. He seemed to be enveloped in a white toweling robe, with the hood up, and he held an enormous white handkerchief to his face. Even his skin was a sickly white. The only color was the blue of his eyes.

"Cameron," he said. His voice was unnaturally deep and phlegmy. Ricks's face glistened with sweat. A huge sneeze convulsed him, his entire body curving around the white handkerchief. "It's —" He sneezed again and wheezed. "It's over. Got the job done."

A convulsive cough gripped him, long and hacking. Tears streamed from his eyes as he clasped the handkerchief to his face.

Elle came to stand by Bennett's side, a hand on his shoulder.

It took all of Bennett's considerable self control not to place his hand over hers. In his head, they were a couple, no doubt about it. He didn't want to hide that. If anything, he wanted to shout it out to the world, immensely proud.

But Ricks was a client, and an old-school client at that. He'd find out soon enough that Elle and Bennett were together. No point beating him over the head with it now, when he was in turmoil.

"Mr. Ricks?"

A thunderous sneeze. Clifford Ricks nodded over his huge handkerchief, wheezed, and waved at someone off-screen. A man stepped forward. Early forties, dressed in a short-sleeved white shirt, tie, blue and gold shoulder epaulets. He nodded to Ricks, who waved at the screen.

The man murmured something to Ricks and helped him out of the seat with a solicitous hand to his elbow. They waited while Ricks and the man disappeared behind a door. When the man came back he stood in front of the screen, hands clasped in front of him in a modified parade rest.

He nodded. "I'm Captain Alain Durand," he said, with a slight accent. "Skipper of the *Get Rich Quick III*. Mr. Ricks is very ill with flu and requires bed rest."

Elle leaned forward, frowning. "For heaven's sake, can't you get him to a doctor? Or have a doctor brought on board?"

Captain Durand frowned back. "Mr. Ricks is, as you might be aware, ma'am, very strong minded and has refused all medical assistance, beyond some paracetamol that I found in a first aid kit. The chef has prepared numerous hot soups but he hasn't taken more than a couple of spoonfuls. He refuses all help until you are brought on board to him, miss. There is no reasoning with him."

Polite speak for Clifford Ricks was a stubborn son of a bitch. Which Bennett already knew.

Elle's hand tightened on Bennett's shoulder. "He wants me?"

The skipper gave a brief nod. "Yes, ma'am. Won't hear about calling a doctor until you are on board. I have been empowered to tell Mr. Bennett Cameron that 'the situation is resolved' and that the 'contract is terminated'. Those exact words." His eyes changed line of sight. "Are you Mr. Cameron, sir?"

"Yes." Bennett nodded. Not liking any of this but helpless to change anything.

"What is your present location, sir?"

"London," Bennett said curtly. Trying to think of a reason why Elle shouldn't go to her father, and failing.

"Excellent," the captain said, without smiling. "We are currently in the English Channel and can be at the mouth of the Thames in twenty minutes."

The captain leaned forward, typing on a keyboard Bennett couldn't see. He straightened, looking straight at the camera of the monitor. "I have booked a berth at Canary Wharf. We will be there in two hours. Mr. Ricks would be very grateful if Dr. Castle could be escorted to the coordinates that are appearing on your monitor now at her earliest convenience."

He stood at attention, staring ahead with no expression whatsoever. In a bar along the bottom of the monitor were coordinates. Bennett recognized them as being London area coordinates and they no doubt corresponded to the exact berth Ricks, or rather his captain, had booked at Canary Wharf.

There was really only one answer. Much as he hated it.

"Of course." He wanted to say more but his throat had suddenly seized. He glanced up at Elle.

"I'll be there," she said, looking straight into the monitor. She had her cellphone in hand. "I have my father's number. I'll call when we're there."

The man nodded, reached out and closed the connection.

Silence.

Long, awful silence.

Elle put her hand on his shoulder and he reached up to cover her hand with his. Warm and soft. He had to let her hand go, but … he couldn't. He simply couldn't. He couldn't get his body to move.

Bennett was always thinking in chess terms. Three, four, even five moves ahead. Always in the moment, but calculating what came next. It was a gift and it had saved his ass countless times and it was what made him an excellent businessman. But now, he was frozen in the moment, in the here and now.

For the first time in his adult life he couldn't cast

his mind forward. All he was able to think of was cuddling on the couch with Elle, watching some fun movie with her, laughing at her snark. He could critique weaponry, she'd have something to say about the irrationality of the plot.

They'd have pizzas or burgers or some other ungodly junk food and they'd have fun. They'd kiss and at the end of the movie they'd go into the bedroom — their bedroom now — and make love. And he'd slide ever closer to falling for this bright and beautiful woman.

Strike that.

He'd already fallen, plop, collapsing right onto the ground in front of her very pretty feet. Stick a fork in him because he was done.

So thinking forward to a time when he wasn't with Elle felt … insane. Why would he do that? He didn't want to move at all. Everything he needed and everything he wanted was right here.

He'd thought they'd have time to linger in their cozy comfortable den. Eating, having sex, solving BMC problems, having sex, working out, having fun, having sex. Days and days of it. God, yes.

He didn't miss the outside world, not at all. The outside world was full of greedy, violent and stupid fucks. Inside he was with the sharpest person he'd ever met, who was gorgeous and incredibly easy to get on with. And nice. Always trying to do the right thing. A class act. He felt better just being around her.

It occurred to Bennett like a thunderbolt that he was … happy. It was a hard word to associate with himself. He didn't do happy. He did content, yeah, when things were going well at work. But happy? Laugh out loud, blood fizzing in your veins, sloppy silly smile on your face happy?

Nuh-uh.

He was a serious man with serious emotions yet here he was, crazily head over heels for the smartest person he'd ever met and who made him laugh. While being hot as hell.

In training, they'd had psych lectures and one really forbidding-looking lady had lectured them on brain biochemistry, so he knew what was happening. Bennett's serotonin uptake inhibitors had crapped out. Dopamine flooded his veins. It was all chemistry.

But it wasn't. Not really. It was magic, and it was this woman.

He felt as stiff as a statue, unable to move. He opened his mouth but words wouldn't come. His mouth wouldn't form them.

She must have felt something of what was going on inside him because she tugged gently at her hand, trying to free it. "Bennett," she said softly. "We need to —"

"No." The word came out guttural and raw. As if coming from his guts instead of his throat. He tightened his grasp on her hand.

Elle frowned. "What?"

Bennett turned in his chair until he was facing her, holding her in the vee of his legs, arms around her waist. He knew perfectly well what he had to do. The contract with Ricks was over, he was to deliver the principal to the client. Something he'd done hundreds of times before.

Only before, he was mostly more than happy to turn the principal over, intact and sometimes pissed at having been in confinement. Principals were usually rich and spoiled. They wanted to survive whatever threatened them, sure, but they also wanted to continue with their lives like before, totally unused to any sort of deprivation. No restaurants, no going outdoors, no traveling, no clubbing. They were usually really happy to see the back of him, because he was no fun at all, just as he was usually happy to see the back of them.

Life was hard. Life was hard and dangerous and mostly unpleasant. He and his men knew that, down to the bone. Rich people forgot that, if they ever knew it. More often than not, he and his men were blamed for the curtailment of their pleasures, even if that was what saved their lives.

But right now? Right now he wanted to hold Elle in his arms forever. Not let her go, even if her father wanted to see her.

He could understand that Ricks wanted to see her, sort of. Elle had been in danger and Ricks wanted to see first hand that she was ok. That was the prerogative of a father, even if Ricks had been a really crappy father.

But Bennett wanted to keep her here, with him, where he *knew* she was safe. And where he knew she was happy.

He tightened his grasp. She bent her head over his, murmuring something. He shifted his head and heard, "I want to stay with you."

Fuck yeah.

He surged up and carried her to the bedroom.

Elle was shocked. This was supposed to be *their* evening. Their first evening as a couple. They hadn't said the words, but she was worldly enough to see that Bennett felt it as sharply as she did. There was a bond between them. They were together.

She'd meant it when she said all she wanted was an evening with him, sitting on the couch, munching popcorn, watching a mindless movie. Nothing more than that and nothing less.

She'd never had that. Had never lived with a man. However short the time with Bennett had been, she knew she never wanted to go back to the way things had been. She wanted to live with Bennett for as long as their relationship lasted.

They'd fallen fast, but they weren't children. She knew her mind and her heart and he did too.

That's why her father's call felt like … like a gun-shot wound that hit both of them. Like a grievous injury. Like someone had sliced them open and left them bleeding.

Elle closed her eyes and held on to Bennett as if she were drowning, as if she'd die if she let him go. He was shaking slightly, this man who'd faced a thousand dangers.

It was dark in the bedroom. Neither of them wanted to turn the lights on. She sure didn't want that because she didn't want him to see her stricken face.

He put her down and kissed her, desperation in his touch.

She felt desperate, too.

Elle scrambled to touch him everywhere, as if she'd die if she didn't touch him. They fell on the bed, hands frantically clutching. She ran her hands up under his sweater because she craved the touch of his hot hard muscles. Could this be the last time they had this?

No!

She rejected that thought with every cell in her body. Her father wanted to see her, fine. She'd stay a day, maybe two, with him, reassure him then pick up her life. Which now included Bennett Cameron.

So why was she feeling this way, as if they were going to be separated forever?

Bennett fumbled with his pants and she slid hers down just far enough for him to enter her. She knew exactly what was happening, he didn't want to wait, either. This wasn't just sex. This was a confirmation of the bond between them.

The sex was furious, hot and hard, an affirmation in flesh. His thrusts were so hard the bed shook and the headboard beat against the wall, faster and faster and faster …

With a wild cry, Elle came and Bennett came a moment later. She held him tightly. If she could have, she'd have crawled into his skin, become one with him.

But she couldn't.

And they were about to be separated.

Ten

They were both quiet. There was so much to say but words couldn't say it. Bennett lay in bed, one hand behind his head, the other holding Elle. She felt so goddamned right, lying warm and safe along his side.

Goddammit! He wanted this for another few days. Few months. Few years.

Forever.

"Yeah," she murmured and he realized he'd said it out loud. Bennett was known for his self control. Muttering things he shouldn't was dangerous. He needed to get a grip.

She sighed and stirred, ready to get up. No no *no!*

Bennett tightened his hold but his cell buzzed. Even his phone hated this. The sound was harsh, imperious, grating. He took his time answering and the buzzing ceased. Immediately after that was the loud gong sound of an incoming text message. From Ricks.

Where are you?

Bennett could add the missing words. *Where the*

fuck are you? is what Ricks wanted to write.

"Is that my dad?" Elle asked, not looking at his phone but at him.

He nodded, thumbing his response.

On our way.

He opened his mouth to say the words, *we should get going.* He simply couldn't say them. There was a rock in his throat that extended down into his chest. Heavy and unyielding and painful.

"I guess we should get going," Elle said sadly.

Why was this so *hard?*

Elle felt like every single muscle in her body had seized up, simply wouldn't work. Her feet felt nailed to the floor and she didn't know what to do with her hands, numb and clumsy. It was hard to breathe and there was a harsh buzzing in her head.

It had been such whiplash, from planning a perfect evening with Bennett Cameron — hanging out on the couch, munching junk food, watching a good adventure movie, smooching, was as good as it gets — to leaving this fun cocoon, going out in the driving rain to meet with her father.

Even the weather disapproved of them leaving

the apartment. Rain slammed harshly against the windows, though they were so soundproofed there was no noise. But there was a gray curtain outside with tendrils of fog, and the sky lit up from time to time with lightning. A real storm, trying its best to tell her and Bennett to just stay in and cuddle.

Why couldn't they listen?

Her father was okay. The danger was over. She saw her father once a year, what made now so special? He obviously felt the same because other than the occasional Skype session on her birthday and his, and Christmas, he was always too busy to meet with her, even when they happened to be in the same city.

But — Elle was hard wired for duty. She was highly self disciplined and nurtured a fondness for her father which he didn't really deserve. Unfortunately, she really felt it, felt affection even though he'd been a neglectful father.

He'd been through a harrowing experience. He'd been in danger himself and he'd be feeling guilty about putting her in danger. It made sense that he really wanted to see her.

So, she was going to meet with him, reassure him that all was okay then … come back to Bennett? Finish what they'd started? Though she didn't want to finish anything. Bennett had opened a door onto a big wide world she wanted to explore for a long long time.

She stood and pulled in a deep breath, like a diver on the high board, about ready to dive in. Bennett was behind her, holding her in a very tight hug.

His lips brushed her ear and electricity ran through her, head to toe. "I don't want you to go." His voice was a deep whisper.

Elle crossed her arms over his. "Yeah. I don't want to go. But —"

"But you have to." He released her, stepped back, and turned her around. She was surprised at his face. He'd lost some color and deep lines bracketed his mouth. His jaw muscles bunched. "Fuck." He winced. "Sorry."

"Fuck about sums it up." She took another step back. There were all sorts of things to think about. It was like her life had suddenly started up again after the 'pause' button had been pushed in Oxford. She had to pack and get in touch with her university, and there was that Las Vegas conference to start preparing for …

She couldn't do any of that. All she could do was stand stock still and stare at him. At this man who had become so central to her life in only a couple of days.

"I need to —" she waved her hand awkwardly, unable to finish the sentence. Basically she needed to get on with her life, but she didn't know how.

She followed Bennett into the living room.

"Just pack a few things," he said. "I'll pack up the rest. When you've reassured your father and you can leave him, tell me where you are and I'll come pick you up. Wherever you are, I'll come for you."

Something in her that was hard and cold suddenly relaxed. She could breathe again. He would come for her.

"Okay."

"I don't think you have my numbers." Bennett picked up her cell, put the battery back inside and started inputting numbers. "I'm giving you my work numbers and my personal number. For the work numbers, I'll give orders to put you through to me right away, no matter what I'm doing." He looked up from the screen, the light from her cell reflecting off his chin. "Listen to me. I want you to call me as soon as you can. Even before you know when you'll be free. I won't go to bed tonight until I hear from you. Okay?" His jaw muscles bunched again.

"Yes. Okay." He looked like he'd explode if she didn't say okay.

A swift nod and he continued inputting numbers. He seemed to have a lot of them. Handing over the cell to her, his hand lingered over hers. "Damn. I don't want to let you go," he whispered again. The words came from some place deep in his chest, raw and hoarse.

She couldn't even speak. Something hot and spiky was in her throat. She simply nodded.

"This isn't over. It isn't even close to being over."

She nodded again. They were both beyond any kind of games. They had something, something real. "No," she whispered.

Bennett shuddered and clenched his fists. "I — I

can't touch you. If I do, we'll never get out of here. Get a small bag ready and let's go."

Elle nodded, went back into the bedroom. Their bedroom. God, only a few days had passed and already she had better memories of this room than she did of her bedroom back home in Boston, where she'd lived for seven years.

She changed into a cashmere sweater, wool pants, ankle boots, took the big down coat off the hanger and then just stared at the closet full of fun, colorful clothes. She'd gone to town with the orders. She'd been angry and resentful and had spent a lot of money. Though as Bennett pointed out, her dad had tons of money, no problem. He would never even feel it. He had way too much for his own good and it had cost him everything valuable in life. But in a roundabout way, his greed had brought her to Bennett and that made up for a lot.

No use packing much, she wouldn't be staying long on her father's yacht. One night, maybe two if he was really shaken.

She put in another sweater, another set of underwear, pajamas, slippers, her beauty case, a cashmere shawl, placed the down coat over her arm, and she was ready. Not happy to leave, but bracing herself to do so.

Bennett looked up as she stood on the threshold of the bedroom. They both froze as an invisible stream of energy blazed between them. Elle was afraid to move, afraid to break that energy. It almost felt like it was the only thing holding her upright.

How silly to feel like this. So lost and bereft. So unlike her.

He broke the silence. "You'll call me the instant you can." It wasn't a suggestion. It was also the tenth time he'd said it.

She nodded, heart in her throat.

"Say it."

"I'll call you as soon as I can."

"And I'll come get you."

She nodded.

"*Say it.*"

"You'll — you'll come as soon as you can. To get me."

"That's right. Wherever you are. I don't care, I'll be there."

Elle clapped the back of her hand over her mouth to stifle a sob that rose swiftly from her chest. *Do not cry, do not cry,* she told herself fiercely. There was absolutely nothing to cry about. Why was she behaving like this?

He was about to take a step forward, but stopped himself. "Are you packed?"

She nodded, unable to speak, stepping aside to show the small carry-on she'd packed. He grabbed the handle and gestured for her to go ahead to the front door.

In the hallway, Bennett morphed immediately into Super Security Guy, body tense and alert, eyes checking everything. He held her carry-on in his left hand and kept his right hand free, not even touching her.

He was armed. She'd seen the shoulder holster under his jacket.

The danger was over but for some reason Bennett was still on high alert.

She felt on high alert too, but for a different reason. She felt like something important was ending and she had to commit these last fleeting moments to memory. Which was ridiculous. He'd spent the past hour repeating endlessly that they'd be back together soon.

Why was she feeling like this? It was beyond her. She wasn't a fanciful woman, she wasn't given to feelings of gloom and doom, but here she was, feeling like a woman going to her own execution.

They didn't speak in the elevator, both staring straight ahead. She could see them in the polished brass of the elevator doors, both with grim faces and tense stances.

The elevator passed the lobby level, passed the spa level and continued down to the garage. The doors opened onto a cavernous pristine white area. She'd been here before, obviously, but had no memory. She'd been drugged.

It felt like a million years ago.

Elle was walking slowly but Bennett kept pace with her, step by step, showing no signs of impatience. She simply couldn't walk more quickly. Her steps echoed in the vast underground parking garage, sounding a slow dirge. Somehow, Bennett was making no noise at all, though he was wearing boots just like her.

Bennett reached into his jacket pocket and a big dark blue car made a sound like an animal recognizing its master, lights flashing. He opened the passenger side door, settled her in, then got into the driver's seat. Elle had no idea what make the car was, but it was a luxury car, smelling of leather and power.

They pulled out, making for the ramp, then exited onto the street.

It was as if she'd been living in a black and white movie and suddenly color switched back on. She'd forgotten about the world, but here it was in all its garish glory, lights and movement and people. It had been easy to forget about the world in her sound-proofed beige cocoon, but now there was a huge dizzying burst of lights and movement. All silent.

No sounds penetrated the luxurious car. Doubtless it was soundproofed and possibly bullet proof. But all the lights and colors of London were there.

They were on the Strand and Elle looked out the window, watching the restaurants, theaters, shops stream by. All brightly lit, all bustling with people. It was dark and the street lamps were lit.

No surprise, Bennett was a great driver. She recognized good driving because she was a terrible driver herself. She'd barely passed her driver's license test on the third try and drove as little as possible. And driving on the *left?* No way. Driving on the right was bad enough.

But he handled the big car like a boss.

"Where are we headed?" The sound of her voice was almost shocking in the silence. Bennett never took his eyes off the road, but he did lift his hand from the gearshift on the console to pick her hand up and bring it to his mouth.

"Canary Wharf. The Isle of Dogs. That's where your father booked a berth, remember?"

"I don't know London that well. I've never been to Canary Wharf. Don't even know where it is."

"Well no surprise if you've never been there. It's a new development about a mile and a half downriver from here. We'll be there in about half an hour, depending on traffic. Are you tired? Do you want to take a little nap?"

She shook her head.

A nap? And miss these last minutes with Bennett? She looked at his hard profile hungrily. No way.

God. *Last minutes.* Where did that come from? They'd already made plans to meet again, as soon as possible. Bennett was backing away out of respect for her father, but he wasn't backing away forever. He'd made that more than clear. They'd see each other again soon.

But somehow Elle was mired in sadness, an emotion so alien to her she hardly recognized it. Maybe she was tired. That was it. Though she'd been tired before — she often worked through the day and night to exhaustion — this sad and desolate mood had never happened to her. It wasn't usual and it wasn't warranted, but there it was.

She sighed and resigned herself to getting through the next half hour, then the following hours with her father, reassuring him she was all right, maybe listening to his version of what had happened. Counting the minutes until she could get back to Bennett.

Wow. Had he slipped some love potion into her drink? She glanced again at his grim, set profile, not the look of a gentle lover. If anything, he looked pissed off. Not at her, but at the circumstances.

She sighed. He was definitely a man you could love, though. Elle used that term for the first time inside her head as referred to a human being, particularly of the male persuasion. Up until now she'd used it mainly for pizza and math.

Did she love Bennett? It felt an awful lot like love, though she was only familiar with the feeling second-hand. Books and movies, the go-to emotional coaches of single women. The addictive rush of emotion when she saw him or even thought of him, that was exactly what the books described.

Was it sex? Probably. Certainly it was the best sex she'd ever had and infinitely better than anything she'd thought possible. But Bennett was no stud. Or at least not just a stud. He was a strong and honorable man, thoughtful and smart and kind, while being savvy about the way the world worked in a way she deeply admired.

She herself wasn't too savvy about the world, she

knew that. She'd always preferred the academic to the practical. Working with him on real world solutions to real world problems had been thrilling.

But she was also aware of the fact that she was at several removes from what he'd had to face as a soldier. She could never have done that and come out sane the other end. He had. He'd faced blood and death and hadn't come out jaded and cynical.

They were driving down twisted narrow streets. Bennett drove unerringly, the way London taxicab drivers did, which always astonished her when she was in the city. Most American cities were complex, but were basically a big grid. Not London, which had at its heart narrow crooked lanes. She always got lost when she was here. But then she didn't have much of a sense of direction.

"Where does your dad want to take you?" His deep voice broke the silence.

Elle blinked. She hadn't even thought of that. "I — I don't know. He won't want to take me to his headquarters in New York, not on the yacht. He has offices in Paris and Amsterdam. But bottom line — I don't know. I don't know my father all that well. It's only recently that we've been communicating more. But I don't know the man. Not really. I know my step dad much better than I do him."

Without moving his head, Bennett shifted his eyes to her. She sighed.

"I know what you're thinking. Yes, he's been a terrible dad. And he was a terrible husband. I don't remember much about him from when I was small. My mom married my step dad when I was eight and he raised me. He was a great dad to me. My father — my biological father — is more like an elderly uncle you rarely see. So, bottom line — I have no idea where he wants to take me."

It began to rain harder, the sky dark and low. A flash of sheet lightning flickered and water poured onto the city, sluicing down cobble-stoned streets, bouncing off awnings, drumming loudly on the car roof.

Great. Not even the weather wanted her to leave.

She so fiercely wanted to be back in Sparrow Square, warm and snug with Bennett on the couch, watching Tom Cruise do his thing, knowing she was leaning against the very strong body of the real deal, not an actor playing a part. Someone who could take down terrorists for real.

The rain picked up its tempo, cutting visibility down to a few feet.

She saw something steely gray at the end of a street and realized that they'd reached the Thames again. He'd cut through the heart of the medieval city.

"We're close," Bennett said and the air in the car grew even heavier. Elle didn't have that much expertise in flirting and in relationships, but if this were a romantic comedy, they'd be laughing and smiling, reminiscing about the good times they'd had. Happily planning to get back together again as soon as they could.

Cool and relaxed, the troubles over.

This didn't feel like that at all. This felt like … like the exchange of prisoners on Bridge of Spies, where you didn't know if you'd make it across the bridge.

Bennett turned onto a narrow street that was more an embankment than a street. Right at river level. They rolled up to a gate with a guard in a hut. Bennett buzzed down his window, not blinking at the cold and rain that swept in.

"Bennett Cameron for Mr. Clifford Ricks," he said. The arm across the road clanked and started lifting.

The guard touched the rim of his hat. It was dark blue with the name of the marina stitched across it in gold. "Slip 4G sir," he said.

Bennett nodded and the window rolled silently back up.

They drove along the marina. There were several yachts there but of course the largest and flashiest was her father's. He had three of them, one berthed in Florida year round, one berthed in Amsterdam and one berthed in Singapore. She had never been on this one before, the Amsterdam one, but she'd seen pictures. The *Get Rich Quick III*, which more or less summed up her father's life philosophy.

Intense flashing light lit up the marina and the yacht and two seconds later thunder boomed.

Elle kept her face expressionless, her body language still. With every fiber of her being she did not want to get on to that yacht. She'd been on previous yachts he'd owned and they were all garish and over the top. Almost embarrassing in their extravagance, for a man who didn't enjoy the sea and didn't even know how to swim. His yachts had nothing to do with the sea and everything to do with showing off his wealth.

And though she was really glad for him that he'd solved his money problems and was no longer in danger, it didn't have that much to do with her.

She didn't want to be here, she wanted to be with Bennett.

He was leaning forward a little, checking the GPS navigator on the dashboard, then finally rolled to a stop. The rain drummed on the roof and bounced off the road. He rested his wrists on the top of the steering wheel, big hands dangling and turned to her. "We're here."

She nodded, a huge hot lump in her throat. *I don't want to go* was stuck in her throat and nothing else would come out. But saying she didn't want to go was childish. She wasn't a child and neither was he. This had to be done and she was going to do it.

"It's raining really hard," she said, looking out the window.

"Yeah. And it's freezing cold. I'm really glad you got that down coat."

She smiled faintly. "It was amazingly expensive."

"Good. It won't protect you much from the rain, though. I've got a big umbrella in the trunk. I'll come around with it. You'll be ok."

No, I won't, she wanted to say, but that was ridiculous. Of course she'd be okay. "Thanks."

Bennett nodded but didn't move. He turned his head and looked at her. "God," he said. "I don't want to let you go."

"No." Her voice was a raw whisper.

He took her hand and glanced out the front windshield at the *Get Rich Quick III* lit up like a giant Christmas tree.

"Remember. Call me as soon as you can, even if you don't know when you'll be free. I just want to hear your voice. And as soon as you know where you're getting off, I'll be there as fast as I can come. I'm clearing the decks for the next few days. And then —" he tightened his grip on her hand. "Then I'm not letting you go for a long long time."

Tears welled in her eyes. Oh God, *please don't let me cry.* "I'll call you as soon as I can. I don't know what my father wants or how long he wants me to be with him. I think — I think this has given him a real scare."

Bennett's mouth tightened. "It damned well should. His greed could have gotten you killed. Okay, there's someone on the bridge with binoculars watching us. Either someone in your father's security detail or the skipper. We have to get moving."

She looked out but the rainfall was so dense all she could see was the vague shape of the huge ship, the five decks fully lit up. She could barely make out the figure of a person on the bridge and certainly couldn't tell if he was holding binoculars or not.

"Stay here." Bennett opened the car door and slipped out quickly. He must have been soaked just making it to the back of the car. In the moment that the car door was open the noise level rose to a roar, the rainfall so dense it was like a waterfall.

She heard the trunk open and close and a moment later there was a sharp rap against the car roof above her head and her door opened. Bennett was standing there holding a huge black umbrella, face tight and sharp.

Elle grabbed the small carry-on and got out of the car. The rain was so intense it was disorienting, but Bennett knew where to go. "Come on." He raised his voice against the sound of the rain. An explosive crack of thunder and lightning lit the sky and she saw that they were closer than she'd thought to her father's yacht.

It lit the man on the bridge five decks up, watching them.

"Here we go." Bennett put his arm around her back and hustled her forward. The pavement was slippery but with his arm around her, she wasn't in any danger of falling. They almost ran to the yacht, much more quickly than she would have made it on her own.

They reached the gangway from the yacht to the marina and ran up, Elle holding on to the railing. Though she'd never been on this yacht, she knew most yachts were similar in design. They hustled along the deck into the brightly-lit main salon. When the doors of the salon whooshed shut behind them, the din of the pounding rain abated.

Elle stopped just inside the door. Behind her, Bennett closed the big umbrella with a loud snick and shook it. The salon was empty, just bright lights, super luxurious furniture, a big wet bar and an enormous flat screen.

A door at the other end opened and a figure in a white terrycloth robe appeared, clutching the doorjamb. Her father, looking awful, with a big handkerchief clasped to his mouth. He sneezed mightily.

"Honey," he said, his voice so hoarse she could barely make out the words. "Sorry but I can't stand up for very long. But I am so glad you are safe." He looked at Bennett. "Thank you for keeping her safe."

Bennett nodded.

The sound of pounding footsteps coming down a ladder and another man appeared. He was tall with a white shirt with epaulets and the yacht logo on his shirt pocket and cap. Not the man who'd been on the Skype session, the captain. But clearly an officer. He nodded at her father and said in a solemn tone, "Mr. Ricks, you shouldn't be out of bed."

Her father nodded and beckoned to her. Elle paused for just an instant, reluctant to leave Bennett's side, reluctant to say her goodbyes with an audience.

She looked up at him and tried to smile, but it felt like the muscles of her face wouldn't work. "Talk to you soon," she said, her voice low.

Bennett didn't even try to smile. He just nodded.

"Thanks again, Bennett," her father said. "Send me the bill."

Elle crossed the large salon with reluctance, almost dragging her feet. Her father tried to smile at her, turned and made his way down the corridor, reaching a hand out to the walls for balance. Elle followed, with one last glance back at Bennett. He was watching, dark eyes intense. As she turned, she could hear him speaking with the officer and heard the sound of the doors leading onto the deck opening and closing with a whoosh.

Bennett was gone. She felt that like a spear to the heart, this hole where he should be. Man, what was wrong with her? She might well be in love but this felt like love sickness. She had functioned perfectly well for twenty-eight years before meeting Bennett, she should be able to function now when not in his presence.

She shook off that awful feeling of foreboding and followed her father's faltering footsteps as he stumbled to the end of the corridor. At the end was another salon, smaller, more intimate and less formal, though still luxurious. Clearly, this was where he spent most of his time. The other salon had been pristine, untouched. This one had a cup and saucer out, a blanket thrown over the back of an armchair, an open newspaper.

The couch was being used as a bed, with several

pillows bunched at one end and a throw rug crumpled at the other.

Beneath her feet the deck hummed with a slight vibration. The captain was keeping the engines running. They wanted to leave as soon as possible.

Elle stood, completely at a loss. This was her father, who had just been through a traumatic experience. If it had been her stepfather she wouldn't have hesitated a second. She'd have rushed forward to him and hugged him hard and he'd have hugged her back.

It was entirely possible that she'd never hugged her father in her entire life. She certainly couldn't remember the last time they'd hugged, if they ever had.

This was so awkward. He was pouring himself a drink from a bar cabinet. A crystal decanter with a clear amber liquid, which must have been some kind of light sherry or barrel-aged grappa because one of the few things she did know about her father was that he hated whiskey.

She studied his back. He seemed to have lost weight. Well, stress would do that. And his white hair was long enough to curl against his neck. He had white stubble, which she'd never seen before. He was usually meticulous about that sort of thing. A barber came to his office every day. So that was something else that stress had done to him.

She heard the door to one side open. Not the door to the main deck but an internal one. Out of the corner of her eye she saw the captain enter the room, no doubt making sure she was ok.

This was so awkward! She took a step toward her father and a huge bolt of lightning lit up the sky followed a second later by a boom of thunder so strong the windows rattled.

It unnerved her. This wasn't like her. She was seldom unnerved.

True, she missed Bennett and they were in the middle of an unusually violent storm. But still. She was focusing on the wrong things. Her feelings of displacement, her longing for Bennett. It wasn't right. Her father was an old man who'd been through hell. He wasn't much of a father but she owed him some comfort.

Elle reached out a hand and touched his shoulder. He turned and the smell of whiskey assailed her. She blinked at the man who stood before her. Blinked, and blinked again.

This wasn't her father.

He looked very much like her father, but he wasn't. He had the same features, the same round face, short stocky build, white hair. But his eyes were brown, not blue. He had on blue contact lenses that showed a brown iris around the rim. He was a little taller than her father. To most people he could easily pass for Clifford Ricks. And he'd even fooled her, for a moment. But he wasn't her father.

"I'm so sorry, Elle," he said. The voice betrayed no signs of the massive head cold he'd been pretending to have. His voice was high-pitched and nasal, unlike her father's bass tone.

"Come here," a voice behind her commanded. She turned her head and saw the captain. Holding a gun, pointed straight at her.

The man who looked like — but wasn't — her father reached up to remove her hand from his shoulder. His eyes were sad.

"I'm so very sorry," he said again. "I'm your father's body double, when he has to be in two places at once."

Elle froze, her mind — usually so quick — mired in shock. Her gaze shifted from the man who *looked* like her father but wasn't, and the captain of the yacht who was holding a gun on her. The two facts didn't compute, like a bad formula.

And then — it did compute. The equation made sense and was very bad for her.

The fact that her father's body double was here and the captain was holding a gun on her sudden gelled into a chilling realization.

Somehow the Lipov mob had kidnapped her father's body double, commandeered the yacht — with the body double along it wouldn't have been hard — and got in touch with Bennett. If her father had used Bennett's company often, they'd know how to contact him. And they'd have access to her father's computers on the yacht.

The danger wasn't over, neither for her nor for her father, who was God knows where. Her father's body double had lured her out to the yacht. She was being abducted to force her father into the open. It was entirely possible she would be tortured, maybe even killed.

Everything that Bennett had been protecting her from — here it was.

This was a trap, a trap with very sharp teeth, and she had to act now. *Right* now.

She'd done a quick scan of the room, Bennett's habit of situational awareness having rubbed off on her. Crystal paperweight, heavy brass candy dish, ahhh …

She played dumb, something that was really hard for her. She put a perplexed frown on her face. The first thing she had to do was convince them of her harmlessness.

She frowned and let her jaw slacken. "But — but Daddy! What do you mean, a body double? What is this? Why is the captain holding a gun? What —" She panned the room, turning her torso, the very image of bewilderment. Shaking, off balance. A woman who was being presented with things she couldn't understand. Perfect cognitive dissonance.

The captain gestured with his gun to the door behind him. Elle knew with a sudden piercing awareness that if she followed him, her life might be over. She could not be closed up with that man. It would be the end of her.

She kept her face slack, confused, hand reaching out to her father's body double. "Daddy?" she whispered.

His face convulsed. "No, my dear, I'm not —"

Elle focused her gaze behind the captain with an expression of terror. "No!" she screamed.

He'd have had to be dead not to respond. Maybe Bennett wouldn't have responded because he knew her and knew her reactions. But this man had no reason to think she hadn't seen something.

He turned around and that distraction was all she needed. She hadn't clutched her father's body double, she had put her hand close to a silver statue. She hadn't seen this particular statue before but she knew it was by her father's favorite art investment — Sal Mancuso — whose statues adorned many a rich man's house. They were silver plated with a lead core and the elongated head was perfect for grasping.

In a party game, her aim wouldn't have been as true, but now? Now her life was on the line and there was no way she could miss. She picked up the statue by the head and threw it overhand just as hard as she could at the captain's treacherous head and caught him right on the nose as he turned back to her.

His face exploded in a burst of blood and tissue and she was running for the door before the man hit the ground.

Because there was only one possible place of safety — the river.

Without any hesitation whatsoever, Elle ran to the main salon. The big glass doors opened automatically and she ran out onto the deck into the driving rain. The deck was slippery but she was desperate and had no intention of falling. She was going to save her own life.

As she ran, she thumbed Bennett's number on the cell in her coat pocket. He'd taught her how to thumb an emergency number and had made his number her personal 911.

She ran full tilt at the railing, put one hand on the top bar and vaulted straight over and into the dark river.

The water closed around her like a fist.

Oh God, she couldn't rise! Frantically, she wriggled to get out of her down coat that was soaking up the water until it became like a concrete straitjacket. The damned thing clung to her, freezing cold and heavy as iron. It was so dark underwater. For a second, Elle couldn't tell which way was up and which way was down, struggling not to panic. Panic in the water killed.

Think it through! She thought, but there was no thinking, just sheer terror as she floated under water. She searched frantically for a source of light but there was none, just a darkness that had weight and heft and was danger itself.

Her fingers and hands moved slowly in the freezing water as she desperately tore at the down coat that was now more a shroud than a coat. Heavy, unwieldy, intractable. Keeping her under.

In another second or two, she was going to have to draw a breath. Her lungs burned as she tried to pull it off, tried to hold her breath even a fraction of a second longer, because when she gave in and inhaled, it would be water and not air and she would drown.

Death was there, right there, reaching its sharp claws out to her in this cold wet place that would become her tomb. Her lungs burned, were on fire. Her movements slow, sluggish.

She stopped fighting, ready to open her arms and sink to her death, when suddenly two strong hands grasped her under her arms and she was propelled upward like a rocket. She crested the surface at the exact instant her oxygen-starved lungs forced her to take in a lungful of air.

She coughed and a big hand slapped her between her shoulder blades. "Breathe in, honey," a deep voice said.

"Bennett!" She coughed again and threw her shaking arms around Bennett's neck. He was safety, he was salvation.

"We have to get this coat off you, sweetheart."

"O-okay." Her teeth chattered from the cold and she could barely talk. Barely move. Suddenly, the down coat she'd struggled with underwater slid from her and Bennett let it float away.

She was a strong swimmer but nothing about this had anything to do with swimming as she knew it. The water was brackish and smelled of diesel fuel. It was freezing cold and the rain was falling so hard it almost hurt, churning the surface of the river into a smelly froth. She was moving sluggishly, completely uncoordinated, legs barely moving, shaking so hard she could hardly breathe. There was no way she could have stayed afloat without Bennett holding her up. He was looking around and she did too, barely able to recognize what she was seeing.

They were about fifty feet from the yacht, which was slowly moving towards the middle of the river. It was lit up like a small city, several men running along by the railings, more men moving quickly on the salon deck.

There was a sharp report and something zinged through the water. It took her befuddled senses a moment to recognize what was happening. "They're — they're shooting!"

A heavy clank and a moon appeared on the surface of the river and began to sweep back and forth. A man on the bridge was operating a big spotlight and was casting the light over the water that rippled from the rain, looking for them. The light slid over her coat, angled back. The spotlight was positioned on her coat which danced on the water as a fusillade of bullets shredded it.

She shivered even more. If she'd been in that coat she'd have been dead ten times over.

The light started moving in their direction.

Bennett pulled back. "Look at me, honey."

She was shaking so hard it felt like her brains rattled in her head. His hands gripped her shoulders. "*Look at me.*"

She did. She was terrified and freezing and very close to panic. He didn't look scared at all. He looked pissed but not scared.

"We're going to have to pass under the yacht and come up on the other side. Otherwise we're sitting ducks."

The words just bounced off her head. She stared at him blankly.

The big white moon of light came closer.

"Do you trust me?" Bennett asked.

That she understood. She nodded, shaking.

"Take deep breaths. As deep as you can. And don't fight me. Let me do all the work."

All she really understood was to take deep breaths, so she did.

One, two, three.

At the fourth he nodded at her and took them under.

Eleven

Bennett felt a massive sense of foreboding on the trip from Sparrow Square to Canary Wharf. As if the darkness of the world had dropped on his shoulders like an anvil, snuffing out hope and light.

Which was very unlike him. Bennett never felt a sense of foreboding. And he shouldn't now, either. He was on the work clock, delivering Elle to her father, and while working he never suffered from nerves or strange emotions.

He had instincts, that was true, and good ones. But he could always analyze what he was feeling, and figure out why. A shadow where it shouldn't be, a missing phone call, a lamp out of place — he'd noticed those in the past and instantly realized that trouble was brewing. He was fast and he was smart and he wasn't taken by surprise.

So what the hell was this feeling of dark oppression?

Fuck.

He looked often at Elle during the trip but she kept her face resolutely turned away from him, looking out the window though there wasn't anything to see but a gray wall of rain. Still, he could read her emotions easily enough.

She didn't want to go back to her father.

Which was fine, because he didn't want her to go back to her father, either. He wanted her safe and snug and within touching distance. He wanted to continue their routine of swimming, eating, solving puzzles for him, watching TV and having fabulous sex. That worked for him. It *really* worked for him. They were just settling into it when the call came and interrupted everything.

Maybe that was why he felt so unsettled, so anxious. Anxious. Bennett didn't do anxious, either. He was a binary sort of guy. Either things were fine, so relax, or things weren't fine and you fixed it.

There wasn't any fixing of this. Clifford Ricks had hired him to keep his daughter safe, which he had, and now the contract was over and Ricks wanted to see his daughter, which he had every right to do.

And it wasn't as if Bennett wasn't going to see Elle ever again. They'd made plans, concrete plans which he'd gone over repeatedly with her, to get together just as soon as Ricks was ready to let her go. Elle had all his numbers, even — especially — the ones that weren't a matter of public record. She knew he'd come for her wherever she was, whenever she could leave.

He'd made that clear to her. *Really* clear. As a matter of fact, he wasn't going to personally accept any contracts at all until he heard from Elle.

So this was all temporary. As soon as they could, they'd be back together again and damned if he was going to let her go. They were going to have a long talk and figure out how to be in each other's lives.

Bennett could relocate if he had to. He didn't have to live in London, he could live where she did, in Boston. It wasn't a bad place.

Though, secretly, he was hoping she'd accept a job offer from him. She liked working on real world problems and by God, his company could offer her an endless stream of them. He'd pay her whatever she asked. As a matter of fact, if things went on like this, the company might actually become joint property.

But no talking about that now. She was already spooked, and to tell the truth, he was a little spooked himself about the turn his thoughts were taking.

Serious stuff.

So he was a little worked up when they finally made it to Canary Wharf. He entered the marina and parked close to the berth where Ricks's yacht was moored.

Christ, it was a big gaudy thing. Five decks, all of them lit up like a shopping mall. A living testament to Ricks's wealth. In the darkness, in the pounding rain, it was the brightest thing in sight, glowing like an alien spaceship.

Bennett was looking at well over fifty million dollars right there. Good thing that Elle wasn't attracted to vast amounts of money. In fact, she seemed im-

mune to money's attractions. Which was great because no matter how rich Bennett got — and he was
doing really well — gaudy ostentation wasn't his scene.

They sat for a moment in the car, in silence.

Finally, Elle sighed. Turned to him. Her face was
pale, sad. "I have to go."

He nodded, clenching his jaws so he wouldn't say
what he wanted to say. *Don't go. For the love of God,
don't go. Stay with me. We have something really special.*

"Are you coming in with me?" she asked.

Bennett was unbuckling his seat belt and shot her
a look of astonishment.

Of course he was going with her. Christ.

She smiled.

He got out his super big umbrella from the trunk,
grateful that once he made sure she was covered, he
had some coverage too.

The rain came down so hard it made the umbrella
thrum with noise. He had to raise his voice. "Let's
go!"

The yacht was even more garish inside. If Ricks
could have had furniture made of gold and gold-
threaded pillows, he would have. As it was, it looked
like a movie set. Elle had already entered the salon
and Bennett hesitated on the threshold. That awful
feeling — of doom and danger and general crappi-
ness he'd been feeling in the car — doubled.

But he'd already figured out what it was.

He didn't want to leave Elle here.

He had to, though. If life had taught him any-thing, it was that some things were hard to do, but you did them anyway. Suck it up.

Ricks was really sick, coughing and wheezing into a large handkerchief, just like when they'd Skyped. His bright blue eyes were reddened and his white hair was sweat soaked. Poor miserable fuck. First threat-ened, then his daughter threatened, having to come up with ten million dollars almost overnight … And now the flu.

Ricks nodded at him from across the giant salon and Bennett nodded back. Elle walked across the vast expanse to her father. They left the salon and Bennett felt like Elle had disappeared off the face of the earth. He stood there like a dork, feeling lost.

"Sir." It was the first mate, looking at him impa-tiently. "We're about ready to sail."

In other words — stop standing around with your thumb up your ass and get off the ship.

Yeah. Except Bennett felt like someone had nailed his boots to the expensive tiles.

The first mate watched him steadily, waiting. Bennett heard Elle's voice faintly, a door opening, and her voice was cut off. Gone.

Time to go.

Reluctantly, he turned around and made it across the deck under the pouring rain, off the yacht and back to his car. He sat there, hands clutching the steering wheel so hard his knuckles turned white, but he didn't turn the engine on.

Fuck, that feeling of foreboding wasn't gone. It lay in his chest like a freaking stone. What the hell was wrong with him?

The yacht was slowly pulling away from the berth, pointing downriver, east. The apartment was behind him, to the west.

East. Follow Elle for a while. West. Go back to the apartment and wait.

East? West?

Feeling like an asshole, Bennett switched on the engine, climbed up the embankment and turned east, going really slow to follow the yacht as it slowly pulled out of the berth.

What was he doing? Fuck if he knew. He only knew he had to do this. Was he thinking he'd catch one last sight of Elle? Maybe. Though there was precious little to see through the wall of water.

Bennett's thoughts were bouncing around in his head but his hands were steady as he rolled slowly along the embankment, following the yacht. There was no one to be seen except for the captain barely visible high up on the bridge. No Ricks, and most importantly, no Elle.

Bennett was wasting his time. Canary Wharf was a little peninsula and soon he was going to have to travel north to round the small bay and catch up with the yacht when the road met the river. He was going to waste half an hour, maybe more, just to keep the damned yacht in sight for a few moments, though there was absolutely nothing to see.

Hold on a minute.

Bennett leaned over the steering wheel and upped the tempo of the windshield wipers to get a better view of the bridge. The man on the bridge was short and stocky, dark-haired. No captain's cap. The captain was gone, someone else in his place on the bridge.

That wasn't right. The *Get Rich Quick III* was a large yacht, sailing in conditions of intense rainfall and low visibility on a heavily-trafficked river in the middle of a big city. The captain does not leave the bridge under those conditions, ever.

Had Ricks become suddenly fatally ill?

Was Elle dealing with a medical emergency?

Bennett speeded up, wanting to round the inlet and meet the yacht on the other side, try to figure out what was going on.

His cell rang, then stopped. Elle calling him then interrupting the call.

And then a lot of things made sense when he saw Elle dash out into the wall of water pounding the main deck, vault the railing and plunge straight into the freezing river.

He split into two.

The man in him was shocked, despairing. The love of his life was in desperate danger and had plunged into even greater danger. The river was treacherous and she would be battling the currents caused by the yacht and she'd be dragged down just as soon as that down coat became soaked.

The operator in him was already calculating distances and angles and scenarios as he braked, flung open the driver's side door, shucked off his coat in an instant and headed for the low wall separating the road from the river at a dead run.

Years of training and combat allowed him to fix the point where Elle had gone under, something that would have been impossible on the open sea. But with city landmarks on both sides of the river and the yacht rising five stories above the surface, he knew where she was.

Even calculating the turning ship and the river's current, Bennett knew where she was. He knew because it was burned in his brain and seared onto his heart. Because he was diving down to get Elle and he wasn't coming back without her.

In the SEALs they'd trained to swim for speed and for endurance. Now was for speed. He was swimming as fast as a human could move in water with hard kicks of his legs and strong strokes. When he reached where she'd gone down, he swam two extra strokes in the current, breathed deeply and jack-knifed down.

He'd been timed under water at two minutes, but he'd been still in the water, not diving. But it wasn't how long he could hold his breath under water, it was how long Elle could. Civilians could rarely hold their breath for over a minute. And there was a panic factor, too. If you panicked under water, you died fast.

Bennett was counting on two things. Elle was a

swimmer. This was the furthest thing from a calm swimming pool possible, but she was familiar with water.

And most importantly of all, she had to know he was coming for her.

He jackknifed and dove.

Utter darkness, only a foot under the surface. The sky was black and the far-off shorelines weren't lit up enough for the light to penetrate.

But Elle was here, and he was finding her.

Bennett quartered the vast depth under him, turning 90° in turn, perfectly oriented. He knew where the yacht was and he knew where the shore was.

Now all he needed was Elle.

He kicked and dove deeper, deeper yet, scanning the darkness. Nothing.

Seventy five seconds.

He dove deeper.

Eighty seconds…

There!

Beneath his feet, slightly to the left. Something light colored, moving.

Elle.

He swam there with powerful strokes, grabbed her under the arms, kicking for the surface just as fast as he could.

At ninety seconds, they crested the surface of the river, just as Elle took in a deep gasping breath that would have drowned her under water.

She was disoriented, looking around wildly, flailing, coughing instead of breathing.

"Breathe in, honey," Bennett said. He had to get that freaking coat off her but first she had to breathe. Breathing regularly in and of itself was a calming act. She had to get calm before they could do anything else.

She looked at him, nodded, started breathing in a more regular rhythm. Good. Step one. Step two, get rid of the fucking coat that was like a cement jacket. He looked her in the eyes. "We have to get this coat off you, sweetheart." He took his boot knife, slit the coat off her and watched it float away, a lighter shade on the darkness of the river.

Shouts from the yacht carried over the drumming of the hard rain on the river. Bennett held Elle as he watched men scurry like ants on the deck. One of the deck hands lifted something …

A bullet sang in the river. Another.

"They're — they're shooting!" Elle said, teeth chattering.

Suddenly a loud *clack!* sounded over the din of the rain and the yacht's engine and a huge yellow moon appeared about fifty meters upriver. A spotlight. A spotlight would catch them for sure. The spotlight wavered, moving backward and forward as the operator learned the mechanism and then it steadied and began a controlled sweep.

The coat caught the light and a shooter's attention and they shot the shit out of it. From a distance, through the curtain of rain, it looked like a body.

A man's deep voice shouted something in Russian. Bennett's Russian was good enough to understand — *don't shoot!* The Russian in charge was telling his men to hold fire.

They needed Elle alive and they didn't know he was in the water too.

The no shoot command would buy them some time.

Then something else zipped into the water and Bennett knew they had to get out of Dodge fast. A harpoon. The fuckers were trying to *harpoon* Elle! Sink a spear in her flesh and reel her in like a fish.

Not gonna happen.

The big yellow moon was coming closer, closer …

Elle was shivering violently. He had to get her out of the water quick, he had no intention of saving her from bullets and a harpoon only to lose her to hypothermia.

He held her shoulders. "Look at me, honey."

Her teeth were clattering, her gaze unfocused. He shook her, hard. *"Look at me."*

He'd commanded men in battle and he knew how to put command in his voice. She focused on him, blue eyes shining as they reflected the spotlight coming closer.

There was only one thing to do. The men on the yacht had a spotlight and he couldn't swim them both out of its reach fast enough. They couldn't swim away, they had to swim under. "We're going to have to pass under the yacht and come up on the other side." He could see the yellow beam out of the corner of his eye. "Otherwise we're sitting ducks."

She was looking at him blankly.

The moon was coming closer. Soon it would catch them.

Bennett chose the only other words that could work. He made his voice cold and crisp. "Do you trust me?"

That got through. She nodded. Good.

"Take deep breaths. As deep as you can. And don't fight me. Let me do all the work."

He could feel her exhaling against his face. At the fourth breath he nodded at her and dove, taking them under.

Jesus, the water was murky. Right now, the spotlight that was illuminating the area they'd just dived from was their friend instead of their mortal enemy, casting a sickly yellow glow that filtered down. Bennett oriented himself, saw the darker than dark bulk of the hull of the yacht and swam toward it, angling down down down. The draft was well over fifteen feet and he had to take Elle several feet below that, under it and surface on the other side of the yacht.

It had to be done.

Kicking strongly, Bennett held her, the woman he loved.

That had become apparent to him in a brutally intense flash the instant he realized she was in danger.

He loved her.

He was not going to lose her.

She was freezing cold, frightened, suffering. But she wasn't panicking. He'd told her not to fight him and she wasn't. She was helping as much as she could, even though to her, this was dangerous to the point of insanity.

It wasn't. Bennett had done far more dangerous things underwater than this and had no doubt that he'd come up the other side exactly as planned. But if she had panicked and had fought him — that would have been harder to pull off. Being underwater was dangerous. Even with the fanciest high-tech scuba equipment available, one miscalculation and you were dead.

But she wasn't fighting him and she was being as valiant as he knew she would be. So smart and so courageous.

Fuck. He was *not* going to lose her.

He sped up his kicks, gauged when he could start angling up and swam as powerfully as he could. They surfaced in the rain, the lights from the yacht showing that they were not too far from shore.

The rain helped. It was so dense and so noisy that their surfacing went completely unnoticed. There was no one on their side of the yacht, everyone leaning over the railing on the other side.

The sound of a man's shout rose over the din of the rain and the yacht's engines. They were desperately looking for Elle. But by God they weren't going to get her.

Now it was a question of time. Elle wasn't going to drown but she risked hypothermia.

Bennett brought her close to him, put his lips to her ear. "Can you swim to shore?"

She nodded, teeth chattering. He kissed her briefly. "Go."

Swimming on her own would warm her muscles. Bennett kept exact pace with her, stroke for stroke. They reached the embankment which was raised. Bennett rose out of the water, climbing a stanchion. Once on shore, dripping river water, he reached down and lifted Elle out.

His car was nearby. He had no idea if someone had taken note of the make of his car but since these weren't amateurs, he was sure someone had. Elle needed warmth and dry clothing but he couldn't do it here where they risked being seen.

He helped a dripping Elle into the car, got behind the wheel and moved the car without switching on the headlights. He took a side road and then another to get out of sight from the river. Only then did he stop and switch on the lights.

Elle's teeth were chattering and she was deathly pale.

God.

Bennett always kept a go-bag for emergencies. He had some elegant business clothes but he also kept clean sweats and socks. He also kept a fleece blanket and a crinkly thermal blanket. In a second, he was sitting beside her, stripping her of all her clothes, trying to dry her off roughly, dressing her with one of his tee shirts, a fleece jacket, his sweat pants which nearly fell off her, clean dry socks. He had all the hot air vents directed toward her and had turned her seat warming system on.

He himself was still soaking wet but he knew himself and knew he was far from hypothermia. Right now, getting Elle to someplace warm was essential.

He peeled rubber getting out of there, driving as fast as he could without attracting police attention. Some traffic cams would catch him and he'd get some tickets later.

As if he gave a fuck.

He flicked a glance at her as he overtook a city bus. "I don't have anything warm to give you to drink, honey," he said. Taking one hand off the steering wheel, he brought her hand to his mouth and kissed the back of it. His thumb on her wrist showed her pulse as weak, sluggish. Her skin was still clammy and icy cold. "I'll make some tea as soon as we get home."

As soon as we get home.

Home.

She glanced at him and nodded, trying to smile. Yeah. That apartment had turned into a home for both of them.

He pressed on the accelerator. Until he heard sirens, he was going to push the envelope.

He tapped the speed dial on the automated phone

system on the dashboard. One ring and it was picked up. Something in him relaxed just a little on hearing that deep voice.

"Larssen speaking."

Yeah. Steve Larssen. They'd served together. Steve was cool and unflappable. He could do a crossword puzzle while killing tangos but what was even more important, he'd also trained as a medic.

"Steve. I have my principal with me. She spent about twenty minutes in the Thames and is at risk of hypothermia. Hospitals are out of the question." The Lipov mob would be monitoring all hospital emergency wards. "Can you meet us at Sierra Hotel?"

Sierra Hotel was the safe house.

"Roger. Be there in twenty." He disconnected.

Bennett could have kissed him on the mouth. Five words, conveying everything that had to be said. Anyone listening — though they were on secure comms — wouldn't have a clue. But Steve had everything he needed to know. Steve knew the contract was for a woman and knew what was at stake. He'd be at the safe house in twenty and if he wasn't, it meant he was dead.

A huge weight lifted from his chest.

Bennett didn't trust himself to treat Elle. He had been a SEAL. All of them knew about hypothermia. They'd had classes and drills and hands on training. He'd spent an hour in the waters off the Kamchatka Peninsula in November before making it back to the submersible and then back to the ship and had just avoided hypothermia. He knew almost as much as Steve about hypothermia. But he was emotionally involved and Steve wasn't.

Elle was leaning her head against the headrest, eyes closed.

God no.

"Elle!" Bennett deliberately made his voice sharp. He put command in his voice again. Elle's eyes popped open. "Don't go to sleep," he said.

She blinked, clearly groggy. "No. Wasn't sleeping. Just resting my eyes." Her voice slurred.

"Don't do that, either. Here." He punched the in-car music system. Fuck. Bach. That was excellent go-to-sleep music. It calmed him but she didn't need calming, she needed to stay alert.

Hypothermia slowed the heart rate. Sleeping slowed it down even more. Hypothermia sometimes tipped you from sleep to death in an instant.

Not on his watch.

He found some hip hop music. He didn't like it and was sure Elle didn't either, but it was lively and loud. Her eyes fluttered shut and he increased the volume. She opened her eyes, frowned. Annoyed.

Good. Better annoyed than dead.

Keep her talking.

"Where are we going?"

Under the blanket, her hands opened up. "I don't know." Voice a little groggy. He took a corner on two wheels.

"Think about it, Elle. You're super smart. Where

are we going?"

Her eyes were closed again. "Elle!" She was startled back awake. "Where are we going, honey? Where have we spent the past two days?"

Hell, had it only been two days? His entire life had been upended in two days. He was a different man.

"Sparrow," she murmured.

"What? Where did you say?" Bennett made his deep voice loud and obnoxious. That mansplaining tone that annoyed women so. "Sparrow what?"

She blinked slowly and he hoped she was feeling annoyed. "What?"

"You said sparrow. Sparrow what?"

God, they were close. Another two blocks. He'd driven like a reluctant mule going to Canary Wharf. Now he was like a greyhound arrowing toward the finish line.

"Square." She mumbled the word, teeth chattering.

Though the car was overheated, Elle was shivering hard. Good. Shivering was the body trying to create heat in the muscles. When the body stopped shivering, death was close by. She was actually shaking, which was excellent.

"We're here, honey. Sparrow Square. Soon we'll be home."

At the word, she tried a smile and his heart turned over in his chest. His brave lady. He was going to find out what had happened back there at Canary

Wharf but right now getting Elle's core temperature up was more important.

Bennett plunged into the parking garage of Sparrow Square, the transponder in his car window opening the bar. The transponder was registered to a Mr. Alan Light of Edinburgh in case anyone was trying to keep tabs on him. Mr. Light was a hard man to find. Invisible, actually, since he didn't exist.

He parked in his spot and was rounding the car before it stopped rocking. He opened the passenger side door and lifted Elle out, blankets and all, cradling her for a moment, just so freaking glad she was alive.

Another ten seconds underwater and he'd be taking her to the morgue. He shuddered.

Elle lifted a trembling hand from inside the blanket to caress his cheek. "You — you're c-c-cold t-too."

Something in Bennett's chest glowed warm. He turned his head and kissed the palm of her hand. "No, sweetheart, I'm fine. Let's take care of you, now."

Bennett carried her up to the apartment. Via his cell, he'd turned the thermostat way up on the way over and it was nice and warm. Too warm for him but great for her. He put her down in the bathroom and touched her forehead, frowning. Ice cold. She was shivering in his arms.

He put her gently on her feet and held her with one arm while he ran hot water into the tub. Hot, but not too hot, he didn't want to burn her. But hot enough to bring her core temperature up.

When the water was ready he helped her shed the damp clothes and get into the tub, watching her anxiously. She wasn't saying anything. Elle not talking wasn't natural. Right then, he'd have given his left nut for some snark from her.

"Honey," he said, trying to keep the worry from his voice and his face, "I'm going to go get some dry clothes for you. Call me if you need me."

She rolled her eyes at him, which he took to be a positive sign, and rushed to the closet, grabbing everything warm of hers he could find.

His cell buzzed.

Right outside the door.

Steve.

Bennett had an app on his cell that opened the apartment door. Steve walked in with his medic kit and Bennett immediately felt better. Steve was cool and competent and right now Bennett was feeling a little panicky, second guessing himself about taking Elle to the hospital.

Steve set up on the couch and Bennett went into the bathroom.

Elle was right as he'd left her. She hadn't moved and for a horrible moment he thought she wasn't breathing either. She was still deathly pale, eyes closed.

He crouched by the side of the huge bathtub. "Honey." She didn't react. Her made his voice louder. "Honey. My colleague is here. He's a medic and a good one. Let's get you out of the tub and into warm clothes. While he's checking you over, I'll make some tea."

A hot bath and hot tea should be enough to get up her core temperature up.

He hoped.

"Let's get you dressed." Bennett lifted her out of the tub, realizing that he was holding up more of her weight than he should. He rubbed her dry with a bath towel and dressed her from the skin out. Underwear, a yoga top to serve as an under shirt, a sweater, a scarf, wool pants, thick socks. He stepped back, looked at her critically.

Elle had perfect posture. But not now. Now she slumped a little as if her skeleton couldn't bear the weight of her muscles. Her face was slack and expressionless.

Jesus.

He walked her over to the couch, sat her down, and put a blanket around her shoulders. She didn't say anything.

What was worse, she didn't react to Steve.

Steve Larssen had won the DNA jackpot. With a Swedish father and an African-American mother, Steve had high Scandinavian cheekbones, light blue eyes and fine features coupled with rich caramel skin. His looks were so striking he couldn't work undercover. Steve was a chick magnet and everyone on the Teams knew that if they hit a bar and Steve was with them, they instantly became invisible to women. The female gaze gravitated to Steve naturally, as if he were a planet and the guys around him were moons.

"Steve, this is Dr. Elle Castle. Elle, my friend and colleague Steve Larssen."

She barely glanced at him and nodded. "Pleasure." Her voice was soft, emotionless. Steve crouched in front of her and shot a look at Bennett.

"I understand you were in the water for about twenty minutes, Dr. Castle." He took her hand.

Elle frowned. Had she understood him? Bennett was about to intervene when she said, "Elle."

Steve narrowed his gaze. "Excuse me?"

"Elle. My name is Elle. And I have no idea how long I was in the water. It felt like forever, though."

The longest she'd spoken since he'd fished her out of the water. Good.

Bennett placed a hand on her shoulder. He was so worried, he was acting stupid — and it wasn't like him. He always kept his cool and could always think straight. Except right now, apparently.

"I'm going to make you some tea, honey."

Steve looked up sharply at the 'honey' but Bennett gave him a hard glare back. *Don't give me any grief.* Steve held up a hand. *No way.*

Bennett nuked some water, plonked a herbal tea bag in it and added about half a bottle of honey. No whiskey. Then a couple of ice cubes so it would be hot but not boiling.

By the time he got back to the couch, Steve had risen from his crouch. "BP low but within normal range. Pulse 60. Temperature 95. I expect that to rise to 96 soon. Out of the red line zone."

Bennett let out a breath. She'd be OK. He put the cup of tea in her hand. "Drink that, sweetheart." He watched as she took a sip. Grimaced. "Too hot?"

She looked up at him. "Too sweet."

He grinned. The old Elle was coming back.

"Elle." Steve took her hand, two fingers going to the inside of her wrist. "Can you say a tongue twist-er?"

She scrunched up her pretty face. "Ummm … Peter Piper picked a peck of pickled peppers, a peck of pickled peppers did Peter Piper pick. Like that?"

"Exactly like that." Steve smiled at her. Elle looked right into his gorgeous face with indifference then glanced over at Bennett. And smiled.

Oh yeah. This was his woman.

Bennett spoke without taking his eyes off Elle. "Steve, I want round-the-clock security in the two apartments next door, two per apartment in eight-hour shifts."

He turned his head and looked Steve full in the face. It was an insanely expensive solution, particular-ly for an open-ended situation. Steve, who held a nice chunk of stock in BMC Security, didn't flinch. "You got it, boss."

"And we'll have to report that Clifford Ricks has

been kidnapped."

"No." Elle's voice was stronger. She sipped from her tea.

"What?" Bennett and Steve said at the same time.

Bennett sat down next to her and put his arm around her, pulling her close. She was still confused. "It's okay, honey. But the police have to know —"

Elle shook her head. Sat up straighter. A little bit of color had returned to her face. "My father wasn't kidnapped."

Bennett opened his mouth then closed it.

"I'm not hallucinating, either." Elle looked at him then at Steve. "It wasn't my father on the yacht. It was his body double. That's why I ran. I realized that if I stayed, I'd play right into the hands of the men after him who were on the yacht. I don't know what's going to happen to his body double, but my father is still free. Or at least he is not on that yacht."

"Okay." Bennett ran the ramifications of this through his head.

"But," she said and a smile crossed her face for the first time since they'd gotten the Skype call. "I think I know how to get us out of this mess."

"All ears," he said.

"It's, um, technically illegal." Elle frowned.

Bennett felt his chest expand, with heat and light. Elle was safe and by his side. If Elle thought she knew a way out of this situation, he had no doubt that it would work.

"Illegal? Who the fuck cares?"

Twelve

"So here's a modulated eigenface," Elle said baf-flingly, and four truly weird alien-looking faces showed up as holograms in the space behind her. Because of course Elle didn't use Power Point and a regular screen. Nope, holograms in space.

But his IT geeks were lapping it up. Five of his guys sitting around in the safe house's living room area, taking notes on their laptops. It was Day Two of Elle's promised five day seminar on her facial recognition cloaking program and his guys — even Melissa Sanders was a guy in his eyes — were trans-fixed. They were already mastering the basics and Elle said they'd be proficient by tomorrow. The last two days were going to be trial runs in real time.

Bennett had fought having Elle give the lessons so soon after nearly drowning but in all honesty, even he had to admit she'd made a full recovery. And a bored, idle Elle was something no one should have to see. She was itching to get to work and he knew he'd made the right call.

She was blossoming and his guys loved her.

He loved her too, only in a different way.

He was watching her, understanding a word in ten but also understanding that her program was going to save lives, when he got a quick buzz from his cellphone.

He went into the room that had been set aside as a gym. He was still the only one to use it. Every morning he accompanied Elle down to the pool for her morning swim. He'd paid a considerable sum to the Sparrow Square management board to close access to the pool for 'maintenance' from ten to eleven am.

He still used the zip ties, though.

"Cameron," he said into his cell.

"The body of Vladimir Lipov was found floating face down in the Moskva River this morning. He had four bullet holes in very painful places and his hands and feet had been cut off." It was Sergey Leon, a friend in MI6 who was specialized in the Russian Mafiya. It was a booming business, keeping tabs on the Russian mob and its offshoots. Bennett had let him know he had a special interest in the Lipov clan. Without saying a word about Clifford Ricks, he had the impression Sergey understood everything.

"Charming. The Volcic signature execution. Always a classic."

"There you go," Sergey said. "Couldn't happen to

a nicer guy. Plus, we've just got reports that someone else who is handless and footless has been fished out downriver. We're going to have to wait for the Russians to carry out DNA analysis but my money is on that being Lipov's second in command."

"Wouldn't take that bet," Cameron said smiling. "Thanks a lot, man."

"Sure thing," Sergey said.

Bennett couldn't pay him for the favor, it would be bribery, but he could make a note to get Sergey tickets to Wimbledon or to a concert at the Royal Albert Hall. He'd buy them at the same time he bought tickets to Les Mis. He was officially taking Elle now, maybe next week.

First, though, he had to overcome his irrational reluctance to go outside with Elle, into the real world. It was an ingrained security concern but it was also something else. This past week had been all about enforced seclusion and domesticity. And Bennett had discovered to his surprise that he liked it.

He'd spent his entire adult life traveling, away from home. Originally from Wyoming, he'd enrolled in the Navy and then become a SEAL. While a SEAL, he'd been on deployment more often than not and even after founding BMC Security, he was always on the road.

If you'd asked him, he'd say he didn't have a domestic bone in his body.

Wrong. His body was full of them.

This time in lockdown in the super comfortable

safe house with Elle, watching her work, cooking for her, trying to keep up with her, having sex with her, had been mind blowing. He was even running BMC Security from here, no problem.

Everything he wanted was within these walls.

Soon though, he'd have to go back out into the world with Elle, walk the streets, let her out of his sight for a moment or two, ease back into normal life. Stop the craziness in his head. Because fuck, when he closed his eyes all he saw was the loop from hell in his head playing back her desperate leap into the Thames and her white, unresponsive face when he fished her out of the water.

A couple of seconds later and she would have died.

He shook himself, really glad that his guys couldn't read minds because Bennett was known as an operator, cool and icy and controlled. Not someone who had stress flashbacks and freaked at the thought of being outside the security of the safe house.

That kind of shit was for civilians.

His IT team stood up, stretching. While Bennett had been freaking out at what-might-have-beens, the lesson for today was over and they were crowding around Elle, talking Geek.

It was late afternoon and beer and tea and soda were available and a big order of pizza and sandwiches had just arrived. IT people, he'd found, had a weird relationship with their bodies. They'd ignore hunger and thirst for hours and hours on end and then come out of their tech trance freaking ravenous.

Bennett sat back and watched Elle interacting with the tech team. She was now their favorite person. But she was also liked by the operational arm of BMC. The tough guys loved her because she taught them cool new tech tricks that could save their lives, and she beat the pants off them playing video games, even the first-person shooter games.

Every once in a while, she'd look up and their eyes would meet. Whenever it happened, it was like a kick in the chest.

Damn.

It was time. He'd been planning on waiting but there was no waiting. It would be the same a month from now, a year from now, a decade from now.

Het let a few minutes go by, then clapped his hands. "Okay!" Six startled faces, most stuffed with pizza or sandwiches, turned to him. "Swallow and get out, kids. Time to go home. We've got an evolving situation."

They were nerds, yes, but they worked for a security company. They knew when it was playtime and when it wasn't. Plus he put on his Serious Boss face. Five minutes later they evacuated, leaving him and Elle alone with pizza boxes and empty sandwich cases.

Elle turned to him, frowning. Beautiful face wary. "What's going on? Has something happened to my father?"

Bennett sat on the couch and pulled her down to sit next to him. "What's happened is — good news! Your plan worked!"

Her eyes grew big. "It did?"

The plan was ingenious and one only Elle could have pulled off. There was an easy part and a hard part. The easy part was stealing the missing ten million dollars from the company accounts of the Volcic clan. It was so easy, Elle was bored. Alarmed, Bennett had asked her whether she could steal money from any account, anywhere and she cut her eyes at him and answered — *of course.* That was scary enough.

But stage two of the Castle Intervention was leaving bread crumbs, Goldilock bread crumbs — not too many, not too few — that led back to the Lipovs, making it look like the Lipovs had stolen the money from the Volcics. You do not look cross-eyed at the Volcics, let alone steal ten million dollars from their accounts.

"The two top lieutenants of the Lipov clan have been found dead." He didn't say how and left out all references to hands and feet. "It was clearly a Volcic execution so that means that they bought the scam. You did what you said you'd do. You stole from the Volcic clan and made it seem like the Lipovs did it. And in the meantime, the Lipovs had contacted your father when they received the ten million. The debt was cleared, no one has any interest in him any more. He's safe and you're safe. I heard from your father an hour ago."

Her eyes lit up and she threw her arms around his neck. Bennett closed his arms around her, buried his face in her soft neck and closed his eyes. She was safe.

He could have stayed like that forever but Elle was vibrating with excitement. "I'm sorry those men are dead —"

"Don't be." His voice was hard. "They'd have hurt your father, and killed him if he didn't come up with their money, and would definitely have hurt and killed you."

"You're right." She pulled back, smiled, shook her head. "What was I thinking? They got exactly what they deserved."

"They did." He kissed her cheek. "Now that that's done —"

"We can go out now, out in the open air!" she cried.

He wasn't thrilled at the thought but was happy that she was happy. "We can," he agreed. "Now, as I was saying —"

"You got the tickets!" She clapped her hands.

"The tickets?"

Elle rolled her eyes. "To Les Mis. You promised. Bennett, keep up."

"I did. I mean I will. Get them, I mean. Give me time, I'm an old man. I'm not as fast as you." Bennett pinched the bridge of his nose. Maybe now wasn't the time. But dammit, he wanted this *done*. Throughout his adult lifetime he'd taken a lot of decisions and he trusted himself. Trusted his judgement. This was right. And the time was now. "But there's something else I want to ask you."

She primly placed her hands in her lap. Her eyes gleamed. "Yes."

"Yes?" He echoed stupidly.

"Yes." She clucked her tongue. "Why are you repeating everything I say? I know what you're going to ask. You're going to ask if I want to consult on jobs for your company. Absolutely. Yes. Love to. And you don't even need to pay me. Working with your team is a delight. We've already talked about turning my cloaking program into a stealth program. Make people disappear altogether." She smiled.

Whoa. She was going to get them all arrested.

"Ok. I definitely want you working for me. With me. But this is about something else. I want you to listen to what I'm going to say." Bennett took her two hands in his, sitting side by side with her on the couch.

Elle nodded. "Sure."

He slid off the couch, down on one knee.

That pretty mouth dropped open. Good. It wasn't often he caught Elle Castle off guard. He suspected it would be the last time in this lifetime.

Bennett fished out from his pocket the small box that had been couriered over that morning. He put it on the palm of his hand and held his hand out to her.

She looked at the box in his hand, up to his face,

back to the box. "Bennett?"

She looked so unsure, so very young and unsure. Bennett, on the other hand, felt certainty settle on him like a coat tailor-made for him. This was right. This was the way it was supposed to be.

"Open it." Well, for someone so sure of himself, his voice was a little hoarse. He cleared his throat. "Go on," he urged.

She picked the box up delicately. There was no fancy wrapping. He was sure she wasn't the kind of woman who needed it. When she opened the box she simply stared at the ring.

It had been designed just for her by her favorite designer. He'd moved heaven and earth to have it made and it was absolutely unique, just like her.

Made of rose gold, the ring looked like the Sydney Opera House had mated with a Cubist rose. It had its own eerie and strange beauty.

"Bennett," she whispered.

"You know who designed it?"

"I do. It's stunning."

She didn't move. A drop of sweat fell down his back. "Put it on."

She flicked a glance at him, cobalt-blue eyes like spotlights. Moving slowly, she put it on her finger. The right one, thank God. Or rather the left one, which was the right one. She held her left hand out and they both looked at the ring. It glowed against her skin.

Bennett drew in a deep breath. "Elle Castle,

would you do me the honor —"

"Yes!" She threw herself into his arms. "Yes, yes, yes!"

*Dear Reader, I hope you enjoyed **ESCAPADE Her Billionaire – London**. If you did, I'd appreciate a review on Amazon or Goodreads. You might also enjoy **CHARADE Her Billionaire – Paris** and **MASQUERADE Her Billionaire – Venice**, two other sexy, sophisticated stories. Here are the first chapters of CHARADE and MASQUERADE:*

One

The Ritz
Paris

"More wine?" Mark Redmond asked, hand around the neck of a bottle of *Châteauneuf-du-Pape*. Beneath his stylish and very expensive suit, he was at heart a barbarian, but even he knew it was an excellent wine.

He watched as Harper Kendall, the most enticing woman he'd ever met, pondered his question.

He could almost see the wheels turning in her beautiful head. It really was a good wine and she'd only had one glass to his three. But—was he trying to get her drunk? Trying to seduce her?

No. And yes.

God yes, he was trying to seduce her. He'd been thinking about getting her into his bed since he'd first set eyes on her on the business-class trip from Boston to Paris.

His company had two corporate jets but he had two teams he was sending into failed states and harm's way. He wanted them to get there rested and refreshed, so he had them use the Falcon 8X and the Gulfstream G3.

Going to Paris for a few days before his meeting with the head of a big bank had been a last-minute decision; he hadn't had time off since forever. First class had been fully booked and he'd been amused when he'd caught himself thinking that he'd have to 'settle' for business class. Especially considering how, in his military days, he'd crisscrossed the world in noisy, cold C-130s strapped to the bulkhead, pissing in a bottle.

In the end, going business class was the best thing to happen to him in a long, long time, when he'd seen the beauty sitting in the seat next to his.

"Sure," she said and nudged her glass closer to him. Mark filled the big balloon glass one third full, the canonical amount. Any less and it would have seemed stingy. Any more and she would have reason to suspect he was trying to get her drunk.

He didn't want her drunk, but he did want her happy.

Being with a woman like Harper was challenging, full of hidden pitfalls. Good thing he was a man who relished challenges.

She sipped, watched him a bit warily over the rim of her crystal goblet. "So, do you know Paris well?"

"Been here a few times but always briefly, for work. In and out."

Her lips curled in a smile. "Plumbing supply imports."

"That's right." Mark leaned back and watched her. He always chose the most boring jobs possible for cover. Plumbing supply importer, accountant, tax software salesman. "Fly in, make a deal, fly out. This time I wanted to take a day or two to sightsee. Do you know Paris well?"

"Yes, I do." She took another sip. "I studied French here for a summer, just out of high school, then came for a semester during my master's. I love this city."

There. An opening. Mark waited for her to offer to show him around Paris. But…crickets. He stifled a sigh. Still, he was a man who knew how to make his own opportunities.

"Maybe some other evening you'd have dinner with me. After work. You're here for research, right?"

"Mmm." She smiled. "Some business and some research."

"For that book?" His gorgeous princess had written and published one book and was writing her second, which he really admired. Mark couldn't write a book to save his life. He could kill a man at a thousand yards, but he couldn't write a book.

The smile grew. "That's right. Linking historical political movements to architectural styles. I'm keeping it accessible though, not a cultural tract. Are you interested in architecture, Mark?"

He sat back. "I can't say I'm particularly knowledgeable about architecture and its history. I'll happily read your first book, though. It sounds really interesting."

"Well, that's kind. You don't have to do that."

"I want to." And he did.

"I'll write down the title for you."

He deliberately didn't smile. "The title has three words in it. I think can remember them. So—how about dinner tomorrow evening?"

She didn't answer, just looked at him. Mark understood exactly what was happening. She was consulting her internal self on whether she wanted a second date and the only intel she had on him was what he was giving her. He couldn't tell her who he really was, but he could give her his essence.

He was a good guy. He wasn't going to hurt her. He wanted sex with her badly, more than any woman he could ever remember, but it had to be mutual and he'd treat her well.

He couldn't say that in words but he could show her via his body language. So he sat very, very still, and watched her face. He was probably emitting pheromones by the ton because she was just so god-damn luscious, and he'd had a semi hard-on all through dinner, but that was okay. She had to know he desired her. They'd been in constant contact since they'd first boarded that flight and though he'd been respectful, he'd also made it clear that he was attract-ed.

Putting it mildly.

She was, too. This was a strong-minded woman and she wouldn't be sitting here having dinner with him at the Ritz if she didn't want to be.

She sighed. "Dinner tomorrow evening? I don't know when I'll finish up with my work."

"Doesn't make any difference," he answered. "I don't have a timetable. I came in early to rest and to sightsee a little." He shrugged. "I've been working really hard lately, and I decided to just relax for a day or two. So I can work around your schedule, no problem."

Harper made a little humming sound, as if think-ing over reasons to say no. But she really wanted to say yes. She was a real beauty, so she'd probably spent half her life saying no to men, decisively. She wouldn't be humming if it was a decisive "no".

She looked at their table, at the remains of an excellent meal, at the elegant room. Everyone dressed up, the waiters the most elegant of all, low voices, the gleaming crystal glasses, the chandeliers like crystal clouds, everyone smiling in their comfortable upholstered settees.

It was a feast for all the senses.

"Okay, but not at the Ritz. And it's on me next time."

"Not a chance, but nice try," Mark said. "And we can go anywhere you want. I'm not fussy."

He wasn't. He'd once lived for three weeks on MREs—gummy tubes of nutrients that tasted like cardboard, no matter what the label said. He hadn't liked it but he'd done it.

"We'll see then. Do you want to enter my cell number in your cell?"

"No need." He rattled off her ten-digit number. "You gave me your card on the plane, remember?"

She blinked. "Wow. You have quite a memory if you remember it from my business card."

He shrugged. "I'm good with numbers. My business is figures on spreadsheets. A little less interesting than your business."

She smiled. "I love what I do. So, what do you know about architecture?"

"Not much." He knew nothing about architecture, but he did know a lot about buildings. Particularly how to blow them up. "But I'd love to learn."

She looked around. "This building, for example. The façade dates back to the early eighteenth century and it's part of the seamless Place Vendôme. It's said that this hotel was the first in the world to offer en-suite bathrooms."

He shook his head. "About the only thing I know about its history is that Hemingway 'liberated' the Ritz bar in 1944, gulping down its best wine that they'd hidden from the Nazis, while snipers were still shooting on the outskirts of Paris."

Harper put back her head and laughed, and all Mark could do was stare at her.

In the fanciest restaurant in Paris, possibly in the world, Harper Kendall was the classiest, most beautiful woman there. He watched as she tipped her head back slightly, exposing that long, slim neck, and gave a genuine laugh. It wasn't meant to entice him, she was genuinely amused. But God, she enticed him.

Tilting her head made that shiny mass cascade over her shoulders. Those light gray cat's eyes narrowed as she laughed and she simply took his breathe away.

Though Mark was used to hiding his feelings, something of what was going on inside of him—maybe a sudden surge of testosterone—made her still and look at him, startled and then wary.

One of the many waiters started walking toward them with the dessert menu in his hand. Mark caught his eye and made a subtle gesture with his hand.

Not now.

You didn't get to be a waiter at the Ritz by being a fool. A simple nod of the head and the waiter faded away.

Mark had other plans for dessert.

He leaned forward slowly. "I know it sounds pedestrian, but I'd really like a Crêpe Suzette for dessert. How about you?"

He kept his voice even, trying to keep himself under control.

"Crêpes Suzette wasn't on the dessert menu. There was pineapple ravioli with wasabi yogurt sauce and Bresse cheese with red onion marmalade." She smiled at him. "I have a good memory too, just not for numbers."

"No, I meant Crêpes Suzette somewhere else. My room, here at the Ritz." Mark covered her slender hand with his. She was acting cool, but her hand was trembling slightly. "It's on the room service menu. And we could pair it with some more champagne or some Grand Marnier."

She looked at him, her luscious mouth slightly open. Silvery-gray eyes wary.

He waited.

She wasn't saying no.

She wasn't saying yes, either.

He kept his hand over hers. It was warm and soft, fingers long and elegant.

Mark's voice was low, without urgency, though desire prickled through his veins. "I have a suite. We could sit and talk in private." He looked around the beautiful room, full of customers. "Where no one could bother us."

He tightened his hold on her hand, but just slightly. He had big strong hands and he didn't want to hurt her or make her feel coerced. She watched him silently, hand still slightly trembling under his.

"I promise you that nothing will happen that you don't want to happen. If all you want is a Crêpe Suzette and a glass of champagne or Grand Marnier and a chat, that's fine. I'll take it and I'll be happy. But I won't hide from you that I'd like more."

She still didn't say anything. Just sat there, eyes looking into his, darting back and forth, making little silver flashes like lightning.

"Your call." Then Mark shut up.

Maybe more words would convince her. She was a writer, eloquent words probably mattered to her. But he didn't have eloquence in him. He was a straightforward kind of guy. He'd said what he needed to say. He'd told her he wanted her. If he elaborated on that, said that he was burning up with desire, that he wanted her like he wanted his next breath, he might scare her away.

Also, he'd made it clear that she could trust him. And she could, even if it killed him.

He waited to see what she would say. He couldn't remember wanting anything more than he wanted her. Like the song said, every move she made fascinated him. His entire body was tense, waiting for her response. He was tense between his legs, too. He had to will the hard-on down by thinking of Afghanistan, thinking of the men who died or were maimed there.

It was hard though. Afghanistan was now seven thousand miles and years away but Harper was right here, right now. She was a stunner with light brown hair that turned silver in the light, matching her silvery-gray eyes with a dark blue rim. They nearly glowed in the dark. She had a heart-shaped face with silky-smooth pale skin and a mouth that was made for kissing. All this paired with small, perfect breasts, a tiny waist and long legs.

But more than that she was smart, with a dry sense of humor and a bottomless fund of knowledge of the world. He'd never met anyone quite like her, and he wanted her so much it made his hands itch and his dick twitch.

He wanted to make love to her, but it had to be mutual. She had to want it too. He'd rather tear out his own throat than hurt her or force her.

She still didn't say anything, but he could see her rolling the idea around in that beautiful head of hers. That was okay. He was a patient man. He could wait. And for her? For her, he'd wait a long, long time.

Now that she was in his head, he couldn't even imagine desiring someone else. She was everything he could possibly want in a woman. Smart, classy, gorgeous.

She waited for a beat. Two.

Then she twisted her hand under his.

For a horrific moment, Mark thought she was going to pull her hand away, get up and walk out.

But no.

Her palm came to rest against his palm and her fingers clasped his.

His heart gave a sharp thump in his chest.

It was a yes.

One

Boston, ten years ago

Calvin Burns stroked the beautiful back of the woman he loved, Anya Voronova. It was snowing outside his miserable, shabby dump of a studio apartment, the white mantle covering the overfilled dumpsters, filling in the cracks in the sidewalk, softening the smell of rot and mold.

But inside his room was magic. He didn't see the sagging bed, plyboard desk, scratched appliances. With Anya in the room, it was like being in a palace housing the rarest of treasures. Her naked body on his cheap rumpled bed glowed like the finest ivory. Her long blonde hair rippled down her back, gleaming gold.

Fuck, *listen to him*.

Cal was an engineer. Engineers were bound by facts and equations and hard cold math. If his profs or students in the post grad engineering classes he taught could read his mind right now, they'd freak. Cal Burns did math. Cal Burns didn't do poetic.

But then, nobody else had Anya Voronova as a lover. She'd inspire a gorilla to poetry. She was like winning the lottery and discovering the cure for cancer and inventing computers all wrapped up in one winning package.

He tapped out *We are the Champions* on her satiny back, right above the dimple over her perfect ass.

"Mmm." She made a throaty sound of pleasure.

"Like that, do you?" Cal asked. He didn't have to ask. Anya always made her pleasure — and displeasure — known. She didn't play games. He loved that about her.

But then, he loved everything about her.

She smiled at him over her shoulder, light blue eyes gleaming. "Do you know who used to do that?"

Cal froze. "Do what?" Was she going to talk about some lover she'd had before him who'd touched that perfect back? Jealousy shot through him in a spurt of bile.

"Tapping something rhythmic on the back of a woman. Goethe did that, tapping out the hexameters of one of his poems on his lover's back. In his palazzo in Rome."

Goethe. Cal had only discovered who Goethe was since he'd started dating Anya and the first time he saw the name written he would have pronounced it Go-thee. Luckily she pronounced it out loud first. Ghew-tay.

And fuck if he knew what a hexameter was.

Another thing about this beautiful woman. She was cultivated as hell, knew everything there was to know about non-scientific, non-engineering things. Cal more or less had the scientific, engineering side of things down pat, so together they were going to rule the world.

"Well." Cal sighed, smoothing the palm of his hand over the satiny skin of Anya's lower back. "Not a poet. Couldn't write a poem to save my life."

She chuckled and slowly turned over. Every time Cal met those bright summer-sky blue eyes, it was like a punch to the stomach. She was so beautiful she took his breath away.

He hadn't moved his hand but her turning over placed his hand on her stomach. It wasn't a hardship. That very soft skin covered sleek firm muscles all over. She smiled right into his eyes, placing her hand over his, pushing it down.

"I don't know, darling," she whispered. "In some things you're an artist."

And she moved her long slim legs apart and the hard punch of lust nearly brought him to his knees. She smiled. She knew exactly what she did to him.

One leg bent, one long leg open to the side and there she was — open to him. They'd made love not long ago and she was still pink and swollen there. Glistening from her juices. Cal remembered vividly shaking as he came and jetted what felt like half his bodily fluids into the condom and feeling how wet she was when he pulled out.

Her sex was a living embodiment of their lovemaking, like she'd been branded. He liked that, liked the thought of her being branded by him. Her sex, her breasts … the nipples were still hard and deep pink from his mouth. There was a little whisker burn on the ivory skin of her breasts which he'd feel sorry for if he hadn't loved sucking on her nipples so much. She hadn't complained.

In a deeper way, he was branded, too. Highly sexed by nature, Cal now thought of sex exclusively in terms of Anya. No one else turned him on at all. He couldn't even consider having another woman, not when he had the most beautiful woman in the world in his bed, who was also whip smart and understood him.

And loved him.

That was the real kicker. She loved him.

"Cal," she breathed, and all the hairs on his body stood up. He was already hard as a rock. He was always semi-aroused when around her. But when they were naked together, his dick simply wouldn't go down.

"Honey." There was a slight question in the word. What did she want? Whatever she wanted, he'd give to her. He'd give her the moon if he could.

Her huge, bright blue eyes locked onto his face. "Touch me."

Cal shuddered. God, yes. He reached out and gently pushed her legs further apart. The skin of her inner thighs felt warm and incredibly soft against the skin of his palm. His hands were big and rough. He'd been into martial arts since he was a kid and had had a karate period. He had tough, calloused hands. But he knew from experience that no matter how rough his hands were, they didn't scratch her skin. He knew exactly how to touch her, where and how hard.

"That's it," Anya whispered as his hand rose along her thigh, higher and higher.

Cal sat on the side of the bed and just looked at her, stretched out before him like a feast, legs apart, eyes heavy.

There was some painter from some time in the past who'd painted this painting … he didn't remember the name of the artist, or the style or the name of the painting. That wasn't in his wheelhouse, though it was in hers. She was the one who'd showed him the image in a book.

All he remembered was skin that glowed like pearls on the canvas, the woman looking straight at the viewer, long blonde hair covering part of her body, one hand on her belly. It was a famous painting and if his mind hadn't been blasted by lust maybe he'd remember what it was called, but he did remember the beauty of the model that seared the eyes.

That was what Anya looked like, only she was more slender and her hair was honey blonde not red. But other than that, she was eternal woman.

Cal shifted his eyes to her belly, where his hand lay next to hers. Just the sight of their hands together was erotic, let alone how she was posed. His hands were big and callused from years at the dojo. He could shatter four bricks with the edge of his hand but here it looked out of place against her delicate skin. Her hand was slender and pale, the hand of an artist. Male and female.

He slid his hand further down and covered her mound, like a flesh-colored bikini bottom. She had a cloud of ash-brown hair covering her sex, it was so soft to the touch it felt like a cloud too. Small dots of her juices were threaded through her pubic hair like tiny pearls.

She smiled at him, meeting his eyes, then hers travelled over his body down to his groin, where he was as hard as a club. He felt more blood rush to his dick. It was almost painful.

She smiled up into his eyes. "Just from looking at you?"

"Just you breathing does the trick, princess."

She rolled her eyes, as she always did when he called her princess. But the fact was, she *was* a princess, sort of. Her asshole father, who was insanely rich, never failed to mention in interviews that he was descended from Russian royalty. His great-great- a billion times great-grandfather had been a cousin of the czar a million years ago when Russia had czars. It was in every interview with the man. Anya never mentioned it but her father did. Often.

He was a dickhead. Cal hated him and he hated Cal right back.

Not that Cal cared. Not when he had his princess looking at him with heat in her glowing blue eyes.

She lifted her leg and placed her foot right over his dick. Cal closed his eyes because it was just too much stimulation. Her foot was beautiful too, slender, pretty, with blue toenail polish. She rubbed it up and down him and his breathing went ragged.

He had to do something to even this up.

Cal turned his hand, started stroking her. He heard a sharp intake of breath and opened his eyes to see her closing hers. Fuck yeah. He wasn't alone here. She was wet and pink and slightly swollen, from the last time they'd made love and from her body preparing for the next time.

He watched as his hand stroked her, the wet skin like satin. A finger traced her opening, around and around, lingering at the clitoris. He knew her so well.

Her excitement was so fascinating he almost forgot his own.

Around and around … her thighs trembled.

Yeah, baby.

He slipped his finger inside her, relishing the small cry. She convulsed around his finger sharply and he could see her stomach muscles pull. When his princess came, she came with her whole body.

She wasn't quite there yet, though. Close, but not there.

"Cal …" Anya whispered.

He leaned down, one hand planted on the bed right next to her pale firm breast. "Sweetheart." He pulled his finger out, slid it back in. She convulsed again, a sharp pull of her sex. Her hands were trembling.

His were, too.

"Come to me," she pleaded and it wasn't in him to deny her. Of course he would come to her. He was born to come to her.

He slid a second finger into her silky warmth, holding her open, placed a knee on the bed and mounted her, sliding into her in the exact moment she started coming.

Oh my god, she was so beautiful when she came. He never got tired of it. He wanted to spend the rest of his life watching her. There was a ring in his pants pocket with a tiny diamond in it. So tiny you could hardly see it, but the promise behind the ring was big. He was hers, forever.

She was arched back, long neck exposed. He lowered his mouth to her neck and as his lips touched her skin, she came even harder, pulsing against his dick. There was an electrical connection that nearly stopped his heart.

He pressed inside her, mouth on her neck, feeling the fluttering of her heart. His own heart was thundering inside his chest, with excitement, with love.

Man, he loved her. He didn't think it was possible to love any human being as much as he loved Anya Voronova, his princess. He felt her skin against his, but it was like her skin had been removed and he could feel her insides, too. Her heart beating, her muscles pulling, her lungs expanding. He was inside her and she was inside him.

It was exhilarating and a little scary too.

But, hell, worth it.

Cal held himself still while she worked her way through her orgasm, hyperaware of everything going on with her. Her sex clenching around his, her arms and legs holding him tightly, the way she arched her back and stopped breathing for a long moment, as she went inside herself, completely in the moment.

Then she crested, a sharp moan coming from her, her hips rotating, almost dancing around his dick while coming. He let her because it was a way for her body to be prepared.

Cal could be rough. He didn't want to be, particularly not with his princess, but it was the way he was wired. The only way it could work was if she came and came hard and was soft and wet afterward. So he gritted his teeth as she climaxed, then came down gently, her entire body lax and mellow. Arms and legs falling back onto the mattress, wet and soft inside.

Now he could let loose.

Cal lowered his entire body onto her and buried his face in the pillow next to hers. In his excitement he didn't want to mark her, even – God forbid! – bite her. In the early days he'd been so worked up he marked that perfect ivory skin a couple of times and it had appalled him.

He slid his hands up her slim legs and lifted them and opened them a little, so that — ah — he reached deep inside her. If he could, he'd have touched her heart with his dick. As it was, he did his best.

And then all thoughts fled his head as he became a male animal with his mate.

He retained just enough control not to pound her, but it was hard. Every single cell in his body registered acute mind-numbing pleasure as he moved in and out of her, fast then faster. She was soft and warm and all his. Skin to skin, heart to heart, on her and in her, he moved, heart pounding, barely registering pleasure when she convulsed and came again. Her arms held him so tightly, but not as tightly as he held her. He wanted to stay inside her forever but when her hands moved to his butt and her fingers curled in and she nipped his earlobe — he lost it.

Cal moved as fast and as hard as he could, feeling her pleasure, feeling that he wasn't hurting her but pleasing her, but it was way too much. Too much stimulation — that soft, creamy skin, that luscious mouth kissing his ear, her soft, wet sex like a glove around him ...

He erupted with a great groan, lungs bellowing because there wasn't enough air in the world to contrast the enormous heat inside him, like a volcano exploding, hips making short fast jabs inside her until it was over and he collapsed on top of her, completely spent.

His breathing gradually slowed down and he gained the use of his body back. Every time it was as if he entered some secret kingdom where he gave her so much power over him he had to work his way back into himself.

He did it this time, too. But this time, there was a reason for him to get back in control of himself. He had big news. Big *big* news. The biggest.

His face was still buried in the pillow next to hers and a huge grin broke out, one he couldn't control. He let it bloom because ... *hot damn*. His life — their lives — were about to change.

It was supposed to be a surprise because it was so big he'd been afraid to blow the possibility of it out of proportion with her. They'd barely talked about it because he didn't want to jinx it and he didn't want to see disappointment in her eyes if he didn't get it.

Already the difference in status between them was huge, an almost unbridgeable gap. But he was an engineer and his love for her had built the bridge between them, which existed only when they were in their little world of two. And here, in his slum of a flat. He'd been to her palatial mansion only once and the memory was so painful he winced every time he thought of it.

She was the daughter of an immensely rich aristocrat and he was the son of a runaway mom and a drunk truck driver of a father, who'd cut off relations when Cal wanted to go to college instead of driving a truck like his dad.

But all of that was going to change. Something big was coming up and he had a ring with a microscopic diamond in his pocket for when he'd given his news and he could officially ask her to marry him. He'd have asked the day after meeting her but he'd had nothing to offer.

He did now.

Like in a fairy tale, he and his princess would move and begin their lives together in a beautiful sunny kingdom far far away.

California.

She was working on a double major — Chinese studies and International Relations. She could do that just as well at Berkley as here. Better.

She'd come with him.

But first — he had to tell her his news.

Cal lifted his head then his torso up on his forearms. He kissed her forehead, pulled gently out of her. His dick complained, just like it always did because inside Anya was the best place to be. His dick hated pulling out.

But his dick could take a hike because there was serious stuff to talk about now.

"I have some news," he said softly, trying to keep the excitement out of his voice. Time for excitement later.

Anya pushed gently at his chest, their sign for him to get off her. When they were having sex, she said his weight on her was exciting. But he weighed almost double what she did and she always said that breathing was overrated when they were having sex, but became once again a priority post-sex.

Obediently, Cal rolled off her and she scooted up to sit against the plywood headboard, bunching pillows around her.

Oh man. She was just so beautiful sitting there, a naked princess with flat cheap pillows around her for a throne.

"So." She smiled at him. "What's the news? Is Kreizler going to let your name be on the paper?"

Cal frowned. Fuck, he'd forgotten about that. He'd done most of the work on a big paper on the elastic properties of graphene, staying up nights at the lab, laboriously recording tension and yield test results. Kreizler had made a half-assed promise that Cal's name would go on the paper but Cal had just seen the program for the World Conference of Materials Science to be held next March in Dublin and, nope. His name wasn't on the paper.

But that didn't make any difference now. He was going to leave Kreizler in the fucking dust. Leapfrog right over the bastard who treated him like hired help.

"Nah. He's not sharing. Didn't even have the nerve to tell me himself, I found out by checking the paper online. But, who the fuck cares?" He picked up her hand, soft and slender, and brought it to his mouth. "Because something better is on the horizon." He tried to control his breathing. "I got it. Anya, *I got it.*"

He was trying to keep the excitement down but his voice turned hoarse. He cleared his throat.

She took her other hand and smoothed away a lock of his too long hair. Damn, his hair grew out so fast and he didn't have the money to keep going to the barber. She smoothed the lock of hair behind his ear, still smiling gently at him. "Got what, darling?"

He was looking deep into her eyes but he closed his. He didn't want to watch her face when he told her the news because then … well if she teared up then so would he and if he started crying the Man Police would rip his Y chromosome right out of him.

He swallowed heavily, held her hand tightly. "I got that post-doc fellowship at Stanford. Working with a top-tier research team headed by Habericht, who has a Nobel, and by Loren, who won a McArthur Genius Award three years ago. And that's not all. I got an offer from Benson Labs for a part time job that will become a full-time job after the fellowship. And the salary from Benson Labs will pay off my student loans in the first year."

He gave a sigh that came from deep in his chest. He was drowning in student debt.

This was like a dream come true. Cal smiled, opened his eyes — and froze.

Anya's lovely face was utterly blank. Not warm and welcoming, not happy for him, not anything. Just blank and ... cold?

What the fuck?

"Anya, honey, I —" But he didn't know what to say. Because all of a sudden, he wasn't touching her anymore and he hadn't moved. She had. She'd moved ... away from him.

And, oh fuck, she was out of bed, bending to pick up her clothes on the floor.

What had he said? Had he thought he'd told her about Stanford but instead something else had come out of his mouth? Had he had a stroke or been struck by one of those weird syndromes where only profanities came out of his mouth?

Fuck, no.

He remembered precisely what he'd said. *I got it.* Which was supposed to be her cue to cry out with joy and hug him and maybe he'd get another round of sex before asking her to marry him.

That was the way it was supposed to go. So what was happening right now? Something bad was happening, that was what. And he was powerless to stop it.

His muscles were paralyzed as he watched her pick up her dainty, lacy underwear from the floor. She always dressed simply. Bra, underpants, sweater, yoga pants, socks, boots and finally parka.

Cal was too dumbfounded to stop her, ask what she was doing. That was pointless anyway because it wasn't hard to figure out what she was doing. She was leaving. Instead of spending the night the way he'd hoped, she was going home.

He had just enough money left on his card to order pizzas in and the plan was to snuggle up with her and watch some pirated movie on his ancient laptop. It hadn't even occurred to him that that was not the way he was going to be spending his evening, the way he'd spent so many evenings. With her.

But she wasn't staying.

As she laced her boots he shook off the frozen spell he was under.

"What are you doing?" His voice croaked, cracked.

"Seems clear what I'm doing." Her own voice was cool, controlled.

"You're *leaving?*" The idea was still so strange he had to hear it from her mouth.

"That's right, ace. I'm leaving." She zipped up her parka, flipped up the hood and turned to face him. She was like ice. It was warm in his room but a chill emanated from her.

It was so unfair that she was still so beautiful, even somehow angry at him. The hood of the parka was lined with dark fake fur that looked like the real thing. It framed her face like that of a princess in a fairy tale, the kind where the princess wandered into the dark forest and made the big bad wolf fall in love with her.

Her beautiful face was closed to him, eyes like shards of ice.

What the fuck? *What was happening?*

He was getting screwed, is what was happening to him. And not in a good way. A spurt of anger flashed and he repressed it immediately. He'd never gotten angry at Anya, ever. And he wasn't going to start now. He didn't want to start now.

But … what the fuck?

After staring at him coldly for a long moment, Anya turned on her heel and walked to the door. Opened it. Walked out.

Hell.

Cal stared at the door stupidly. His muscles felt slow, his brain felt mired in mud. He couldn't react. He could barely breathe.

What just happened? Was there a pod in the lavish wine cellars of her father's mansion, eating the real Anya after extruding a fake alien? No, that had been the real Anya he'd made love to. Her skin, the sounds she made, the way she clutched at him … those were all real.

Loving Anya was the best thing that ever happened to him. She loved him right back, he was sure of it. They were young but neither of them were dummies. They'd lucked into true love at a young age but they both realized what they had. It was rare and precious and needed protecting.

He loved her and she loved him. Or, up until five minutes ago, she'd loved him. Then something … changed.

Misery was setting in, a dark cloud of it rising like some dank fog from the nether regions of the earth. From caves and crevices where dark creatures dwelled. His head ached. His bones ached.

Too late, he realized he should be chasing her. Cal moved forward, but slowly and painfully, like he'd just taken a bad beating at the dojo. He was good in the dojo, it had been years since anyone had been able to hurt him. But this felt like he'd been beaten to within an inch of his life.

He'd opened his door and was walking out before he realized that he was buck naked. Much as he wanted to, he couldn't chase her like this. They'd arrest him. So he went back in, pulled up his jeans over his hips, jerked on his shirt without buttoning it and jammed his sockless feet into his ancient running shoes.

He limped down the stairs as if both legs had been broken. Something in him was broken. He threw open the front door of his apartment building and stared out in dismay. As usual, the light over the door and every other street light was out. He never let Anya walk alone after dark in his area. The fact that she had … he couldn't go there. The idea that she'd rather court danger than stay with him was so painful he batted the thought away instantly.

It was snowing hard. Not pretty snowflakes gently settling on the cracked ground, but frozen rain flooding from the sky. He could see her boot prints but they disappeared two feet from the door. Right was a long slog to the subway, left was a bus stop. But she'd have to change three buses to get home. She usually took the subway. But never alone after dark, ever.

Her boot prints went to the right. She'd opted for the subway, which — damn it! — was not safe. Neither the streets to get there nor the station itself.

He took off running. He was a martial artist, not a track star. Cal was powerful, but not a runner. Still, he made good time, following her footsteps until he couldn't any more, the thick falling snow smudging them out.

But he knew the way to the subway and he ran as fast as he could.

She wasn't there. Cal frantically searched the filthy, graffiti-painted station. There were a couple of drug addicts, an ancient alcoholic preaching the end of the world and some tired workers.

Cal stared at the dirty station through eyes that stung, one hand braced against the wall as if he would fall down any second as he anxiously screened every passenger. Even when the train clanked in and came to a screeching stop, he studied everyone who boarded and stalked up and down the platform, peering into every car. On the crazy chance that she'd ... what? Run two miles to the previous station and gotten on there?

Well clearly she hadn't headed for the subway. Maybe she'd doubled back. Probably she'd called a cab. He hadn't even thought of that, because cabs never entered into his calculations. He could probably build a rocket to fly him to the moon before he could cab it everywhere.

Finally, he trudged up the stairs and out into the freezing cold. Fishing his cell out of his jeans, he thumbed her number. It was the first on his contacts list. The call went to voice mail.

The call went to voice mail all night. He must have called a hundred times but he never left a message, not trusting his voice.

The next day he called, then went to her apartment. Her father had bought her a pretty little studio apartment in a nice part of town. He stood at the front door ringing her bell for an hour until the super came out and chased him away.

The super's name was Mac, or that was what Cal called him. He was Polish and his name had enough consonants to sound like a sneeze. Cal and Mac were friends. Cal had helped him with building repairs a lot of times. But Mac wouldn't look him in the eye and pretended that his English had deserted him.

Cal called the mansion, though the idea of accidentally catching Mr. Voronov scared him. No danger of that, though. The housekeeper always answered, assuring him in icy tones that Miss Anya was not there, no she didn't know where Miss Anya was or when Miss Anya was coming back and by the way don't bother calling again.

He sent emails, pouring out his heart. She couldn't hear the tears in his voice in an email. But the emails remained unopened and never answered. Three days later, when he called her cell he got an announcement that the number was no longer in use.

He lost ten pounds that first week and missed all his classes. When he almost missed the deadline for accepting the job with Benson Labs, Cal knew that his future was on the line.

He could obsess over Anya and mourn her or he could get his act together and move forward.

He faxed his acceptance and bought the ticket to San Francisco with the last of the money in his bank account

Ten days after Anya walked out on him, on a bitterly cold, sleety day, Cal packed his few belongings and flew out West, toward his future.

Without Anya.

You might also enjoy:

THE MIDNIGHT TRILOGY
1. Midnight Man
2. Midnight Run
3. Midnight Angel

The Midnight Trilogy Box Set

THE MEN OF MIDNIGHT
1. Midnight Vengeance
2. Midnight Promises
3. Midnight Secrets
4. Midnight Fire
5. Midnight Quest
6. Midnight Fever

MIDNIGHT NOVELLA
Midnight Shadows

Woman on the Run
Murphy's Law
A Fine Specimen
Port of Paradise

THE DANGEROUS TRILOGY
Dangerous Lover
Dangerous Secrets
Dangerous Passion

THE PROTECTORS TRILOGY
Into the Crossfire
Hotter than Wildfire
Nightfire

GHOST OPS TRILOGY
Heart of Danger
I Dream of Danger
Breaking Danger

HER BILLIONAIRE SERIES
CHARADE: Her Billionaire - Paris
MASQUERADE: Her Billionaire - Venice
ESCAPADE: Her Billionaire - London

NOVELLAS
Fatal Heat
Hot Secrets
Reckless Night
The Italian

About The Author

Lisa Marie Rice is eternally 30 years old and will never age. She is tall and willowy and beautiful. Men drop at her feet like ripe pears. She has won every major book prize in the world. She is a black belt with advanced degrees in archaeology, nuclear physics, and Tibetan literature. She is a concert pianist. Did I mention her Nobel Prize?

Of course, Lisa Marie Rice is a virtual woman and exists only at the keyboard when writing romance. She disappears when the monitor winks off.

www.ingramcontent.com/pod-product-compliance
Lightning Source LLC
Chambersburg PA
CBHW031716170626
46808CB00005B/1764